Suzanne Lapstun

Letters From The Arctic

Illustrated by Rosendo Li

THE **BLACK SPRING**
PRESS GROUP

Suzanne Lapstun
Born in Norway and raised in Australia, Suzanne lived
for many years between France, Peru and Svalbard.
Currently based in Rome, Italy, where she works in
international development, Suzanne is fluent in six
languages and writes, translates and performs poetry
in four. This is her first novel.

Rosendo Li Rubio
Rosendo is an artist based in Montauban, France.
Born in Chulucanas, Peru, to a Peruvian mother and
Chinese father, Rosendo graduated in drawing, painting
and mural painting from the Institutes of Fine Arts of
Piura and Lima, before moving to China where he studied
pottery and porcelain-making. He has exhibited his work
in Peru, China and France.

First published in 2022
An Eyewear Publishing book, The Black Spring Press Group
Grantully Road, Maida Vale, London W9,
United Kingdom

ISBN: 978-1-915406-04-0

None of the views expressed in this book should be construed as those
of the author in her capacity as an international civil servant.

Front cover photo: © Christopher Michel CC BY 2.0 (cropped and edited)

blackspringpressgroup.com

In memory of Freddy, Miriam, Hans, Otto and Domingo.

Cue

past midnight
a cluster of sun dogs
make carbon copies of light
halos like glass
refract in the haze

ratcheting up the day
the terns switch hemispheres
born to fulfil
dressed to kill
overwriting my tracks
in their wake

Letter to Rosendo

I'm sorry it's taken so long to write. As usual, you're probably thinking. But this time it's not just laziness or neglect, it's because I'm afraid.

Do you remember asking me why I was so afraid to go back? You thought I was afraid of polar bears. But no. Well, I am afraid of them too. And afraid that I would no longer know how to cross a river, or understand the best way over a glacier. But mostly I was afraid of something quite different. That there wouldn't be the magic. Sorry for that hackneyed term. But I mean that real strange serendipitous magic that has blessed my life on so many occasions. I had this fear that I was trying to compress the transcendence of years into a few short days. Trying to call up – or worse, warm up – the old spells from the silt of experiences that took place decades ago. How could I return? And even when I lived there I knew I only half belonged. We are all strangers, but some more out of place than others.

Then there's the question of writing – transforming life into a series of signs on a page or screen. I'm afraid of doing that too. What is life anyway? Are our lives just fables that we spin when conversing with others? And then when a new element appears we are forced to completely recast the story? And what story anyway?

That's why I haven't been in touch in a while.

Is it possible for a writer to have a problem specifically with narrative? That a cohesive story somehow doesn't encode? Or is it that the linearity of place and time is undermined by the abstract quality of the place I am trying to write about? It feels to me that my narrative has no intrinsic meaning; I split it apart and reconnect it as I see fit. I'm not even sure that this story is about me.

But perhaps the place imposes some inner logic that I can't yet perceive. Even from this distance. Some people are connectors, effortlessly bringing together people in wonderful and unexpected ways. But so are places. Some places are what I call destiny interchanges, crossroads where a chance encounter can take your life in a completely different direction. Where many lives weave or tangle together for a time and then eventually unravel.

Books too connect. By setting arbitrary limits to this non-story, this interval of life mixed up with fiction, I create a sort of grid to hang the disparate yet related images of life and landscape, strange and fortuitous crossings of ways, and experiences of solitude that made up those years where I kept going back.

My mind is still full of questions. What is the nature of memory? And memory of repeated events? In their repetitions, they blend in with one another and become some kind of universal truth. It is hard to tell apart all those years back in the nineties. All the walks up Nordenskiöldtoppen – the peak behind Longyearbyen became my Monday evening ritual. The late night (daylight) parties, before-parties and after-parties.

Now in my memory the weekly walks up the mountain have become mostly just one walk up the mountain, the parties mostly just one big party. A few specific details distinguish some of them. Like village memories: "that was the year of the locusts" or "that was the year so-and-so died just after the harvest". There was the walk where I somehow got lost in the familiar landscape and sat down for a cup of tea and biscuits with the Swiss traveller, waiting for the fog to lift. And there was the party when time slowed down and thickened into glass in the glow of the night sun. But in the end, maybe it is the blur that is real, the ritual, and the memory of the ritual – rather than any detailed reconstruction from diaries, discussions, or careful readings of old issues of the local paper.

This book is a frame, a frail scaffolding perched in the future, many lines of latitude further south. And the broader frame also governs the telling. As I sit and write, looking out over the zinc rooftops of Paris, many years hang heavy in the interim.

I couldn't sleep last night. I think my body is high on imagined – or remembered – midnight sunlight. I dozed off in fits and starts, for stretches of a few hours at most, and then lay awake again. Like when that sun used to drill through my window pane at 4 a.m.

I used to dream of monsters during those white nights in Svalbard. As though I was so far away from the density of civilization that there were no human ghosts – living or dead – to populate my sleep. Just the raw primitive spirits of this abstract world. Wakefulness would release me.

Being awake there is also different than in any other place. My internal hum quiets to a murmur. I am all focused outwards, attentive to every sense. A whiff of moisture or animal that might be hanging in the otherwise scent-less air. The sweat of the person sharing my sleeping space. The sound of the bearded seal in mating season resounding through the hull of a wooden boat. A movement, white against white.

Places are like lovers too. My first encounter with Svalbard was an illumination. I was captivated by the unending white coast that greeted the ship as we arrived from open seas. And each time I returned I became more caught up, came to know the landscape more deeply, to read the weather and gauge the rivers, to patiently wait for the snow ptarmigan to waddle out, or *the ducklings to approach, to understand whether the bear will walk away. No, hang on, I'm lying – I never really got to learn properly about bears. But the seduction of place deepened into something different, not commitment, more like an open relationship that I eventually betrayed by not coming back.*

And places are of course inextricably tied up with human love stories, those that blossomed and those that could have been. And stories of friendships, some long-lasting, some brief but intense.

During those few hours of fitful sleep last night, I had a dream, that fiction was an exciting and dangerous place to be.

I was in a city, maybe Paris or London, with a river and bridges. But there was also something desolate about it, as though dusk was perpetually encroaching, and I realized that the river went in a circle, like a ring road. If I went to the right or to the left I would come back to the same place. A place that looked like the entrance to a long-distance bus station at 4 o'clock in the morning.

I met some young people who had been into the fiction. I realized that maybe I would have to go in there too. It might be a bit difficult to come out again... They were not sure how they came to be standing on the outside again with me.

Thank you Rosendo for trusting me with this – I've taken liberties with you, transformed you into Renata, I'm guessing you won't mind being a woman. In Renata there is a lot of you, but also some of Sacha, some of my childhood friend Lisa, and a sprinkling of a few others. By now she feels almost as familiar to me as you do.

I'll see you back on the outside.

If it's still there.

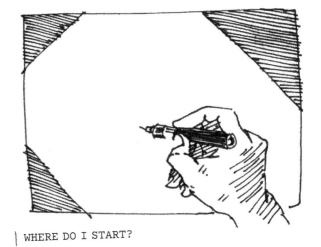

WHERE DO I START?

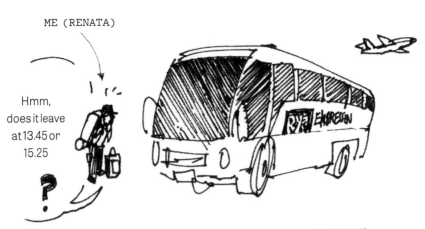

ME (RENATA)

Hmm, does it leave at 13.45 or 15.25

I'VE MADE IT THIS FAR. BUT WHAT AM I REALLY DOING HERE, A PERUVIAN IN THE MIDDLE OF THE NORWEGIAN FJORDS? AND WHAT IF MARIANNE ISN'T THERE TO MEET ME AT THE BUS STATION?

Day 0
Beginnings – letter to W.H. Auden

Oslo Central Bus Terminal.

Do you mind if I address my thoughts to you, Auden, like you addressed yours to Lord Byron the first time you travelled north? It would help me if I imagine you might be listening.

I have brought a bundle of old diaries with me and one book, yours, *Letters from Iceland*, although my destination is a different one. I've been reading but I stop now, check my watch and look around.

Grey walls and white light and hot dogs and sweet mustard. Metal seats, me, and all the others, craning towards the oblique window. Legs scrunched up (I can never sit straight for long), waiting for Renata.

Renata, my Peruvian travelling companion. Quiet, but unafraid to speak up, speak out. Challenging, always challenging, "But don't you realize that everything is political?" This incessant questioning has interrupted our friendship a few times. A hum of anxiety in the background of my mind. We are writing this book together, like you and MacNeice did. Or rather she is driving it, and I am trying to hang on. I am surrendering my inadequacies to her perseverance and discipline.

Travel is political. The Arctic is political. And we all have a responsibility. Renata makes me feel like a dilettante.

Movement, sudden empty seats. Voices, suitcases. "Marianne!" Renata has just stepped off the airport bus; with her lean frame, rucksack and self-possessed air, there is nothing really to betray that she is not a long-standing resident of multi-ethnic Oslo.

We haven't seen each other for months, probably more than a year, but time passed remains unspoken. Exchanges of hugs, stories from the past few hours, the alarm that didn't go off, the smelly man in the seat behind, the sky just dark enough for a thousand stars, older news can wait. "I read the text you sent me about the mountain," she tells me, "with a bit of help from Google translate. I quite liked it, even though nothing really happens in it."

The first crossing (1993)

The ship arrives early. It is 6 a.m. and most of the passengers on board are still asleep.

Sunlight. So much sunlight. I have never been so far north before - my head is aching with anticipation. I have not been woken by the dawn, as here there is no dawn. For a day now we have been ploughing through the choppy petrol-blue sea, following the icy coast, a white line to the east lit by the pale but relentless Arctic sun.

Rather, I am awakened by the change in the sound of the engine, the bumping, the ropes. The sounds of getting ready to anchor. My cabin is quite close to the engine room. I fancy myself a poet who likes to travel second class, although really I don't have a choice.

The quay for big ships isn't finished yet so we cannot dock. The crew get the tenders going quickly to bring the passengers to shore. I am on the first, there is just a handful of people up at this early hour.

The wharf is unlit by the sun, overshadowed by the mountain plateau rising up immediately behind. Just after stepping out of the tender, I recognize a face, peering out from within a thick hand-knitted sweater in tones of grey and brown. "Hello! I had forgotten you were coming up here." The lilting voice of an Icelandic music student from Paris I met at a briefing the previous summer by the man who hired me as a cruise ship lecturer. She and I chatted for a while outside the premises of the French Geographical Society and she taught me the word *tónlist*, or art of sound, the Icelandic word for music. I still associate the word with this first day in Svalbard, despite it being a day marked more by silence than by sound.

She and a young man I don't know are selling books. At 7 a.m. on a windy day in Spitsbergen, waiting for tourists to disembark. The rest of the town is sleeping. There was a party last night and everyone was there.

"Even I am a bit hungover," she admits. "But let's go for a walk. Take advantage of the sun." As no other tourists appear to be spilling off the ship for the moment, she suggests we walk up to the plateau, a steep but easy path up from the port. She leaves the books with her friend and we start up the slope. We should really have a gun to go beyond the town boundaries but we do not. Anyway, she's not even sure if the plateau counts as off limits.

We climb without too much effort and rise quickly above the town, which lies between us and another plateau on the far side. The valley is a gash opened by an ancient glacier, speckled with small buildings like coloured band-aids. And a river, which swells and recedes depending on the hour of the day, the cloud cover, and the temperature in the entrails of the glacier that still broods at the head of the valley. There is no one else up here this morning.

Until we run into a tousled blond gun-bearing type in a red checked shirt who appears with a group of hikers in tow. He looks like a Viking who has just stepped out of a comic strip. The music student knows him, they stop to talk and he becomes more three-dimensional. He turns to me and smiles, "You are so *vrien og vrang*." No, that is many years later. When we are sharing a flat in road 222, and know each other well enough to tell our dreams in the morning and share tales of love found and love lost. I am still not quite sure what he means by those words. Am I twisted and mixed up? Or stubborn and clever, like the princess in the folk tale he is quoting?

The Icelandic girl checks her watch. "Actually I'd better get back to work," she says, and we say goodbye before she makes her way back the way we came. She exits the story here and I don't ever see her again.

"Can I keep walking? Am I ok without a gun?" I look at the Blond Viking.

"Well, there was a bear sighted in a valley near here last week, but nothing in the past few days. I think you'll be fine. The best walk up here is Nordenskiöldtoppen. Just cross the plateau until you reach the moraine, you know, the heaped up rocks and mud at the front of the glacier. There is quite a lot of snow, so watch where you walk and listen carefully for water underneath. Then follow the ridge up the left side of the glacier until you reach the top. There is a snowy patch towards the end, but you'll be fine."

"Are you sure? Even in my Doc Martens?" I look down at my urban footwear.

"Just dig your feet in well."

The peak of Nordenskiöldtoppen stretches up behind the plateaus, between two glaciers: Longyear glacier, which feeds the river that runs through the town, and another one with no name that sits far above the plateau, its subterranean rivers flowing into a couple of transverse valleys.

It is the height of summer and the mountain is a body of rock sustained by a whale-boned petticoat of snow. Across the valley, on the other side of Longyear glacier, I can see the dark rocky outcrop that I will later learn is known as the Sarcophagus.

I cross the plateau, stopping at each marvel I have heard about but never seen. A lone Arctic poppy suddenly waving its white petals in the rocky no-man's land. The realization that the stones under my feet stretch out in roughly regular polygons, formed by the cycle of freezing and melting of the uppermost layer of the earth that floats above the permanently frozen layer below.

The air is piercingly clear and I am alone. Everything seems so close and far away at the same time. In the Arctic distances are deceptive because the air is so unencumbered by dust.

When I reach the moraine, I pause. What had he said about this part? I don't know how to read the signs, and I'd rather not fall into an icy underground river. But somehow the Blond Viking reappears out of the blue and crosses an arm of the glacier unhesitatingly, together with his gaggle of walkers. I follow their imprints carefully. Then he takes his group down the side valley back towards town as I head up the ridge alone.

There are no more poppies or small plants here. Just stones and earth on my track. Rocky outcrops. Glaciers on either side. The mountains are immodestly bare, and the higher I walk, the more they seem to turn into an abstraction of lines, of hard shapes, delineated in black and white by rock and ice. I am filled with awe, or is it fear? I'm scared of heights. I have left time behind me. The light has shifted but I don't have a sense of the sundial in my mind.

I continue upwards and as I do I seem to shed layers of myself. Friends, ties left behind on a continent far to the south. Family, language, city of birth. The ship that I stepped off just a few hours previously - everything is far, far away.

Yet I am scared. And very alone. The path is not technically difficult but it is narrow and there is a steep drop on either side. I decide to sit down. I turn my face to the sun and close my eyes. The shadows of the valley are far below and it is 8°C, balmy for the Arctic.

I am straddling the path, unsure whether to continue or turn back, when another young Viking appears. He is tall and cheerful, and greets me with a friendly smile. I ask him what the time is, a small mistake betraying my rusty Norwegian. "Yes I do have a watch" he replies, "and I can even tell you the time. Where are you from?"

He happens to be the summer stand-in for the governor's Norwegian-Russian interpreter. The rest of the time he lives in Toulouse.

He persuades me that I have plenty of time to climb the mountain and get back to my boat before it leaves, and he will protect me with his .44 Magnum if any bears appear. But he reassures me that they don't usually climb mountains like this. It's a deal. I follow my new spiritual guide as the abstraction continues to open up around me like a tangram unfolding. Each dimension of the landscape seems strangely geometrical, whether you are looking at the infinitely close or the infinitely far away.

When we come to the snow patch near the top I hesitate. The treads on my Doc Martens aren't the best for this terrain. But the sun has tempered the icy upper layer. My guide kicks steps into the crust with his hiking boots and I follow, clamping my body to the slope. I don't look down, but I feel like I am on the rim of a world that I might fall off at any moment.

And then we are at the top. We can see all the way across to the blue and white mountains on the other side of Isfjord. And right in front of us a group of French mountaineers, kitted out with the full accoutrement of crampons and climbing gear. To me their sudden presence is just as surreal as the landscape in which we find them. But the unexpected company is welcome.

They seem even more surprised to see us: a city girl in jeans and Docs and a youthful Viking in khaki shorts with a revolver slung across his chest. Both of whom speak fluent French. They invite us to share their rations of dry bread and salami and we all add a stone to the traditional pile at the top of the mountain. Loose threads of conversation weave through the silence now and again.

"I'll take you down the other side," says Young Viking. "It's easier, no snow."

As we descend, each rocky outcrop looks like we can go no further and my repressed fears bubble up. But then the path becomes visible again, and by the end of it I feel almost like a mountain goat. I don't know then how many times I will come to climb this mountain over the years.

We cross the moraine and then go down Tverrdalen, which means "side valley", which it is, and end up near another part of town, Nybyen, or "new town", which it is not. We are coming back from abstraction, back to re-assuring human structures and messiness. Young Viking takes the bullets out of his gun and slips them into his pocket. I record the ritual in my mind.

Back when Nybyen was the new part of town, it housed the miners, who were the mainstay of the community when coal mining started back in the early 1900s. Now it is home to a mixed population of students, scientists, miners and tourists. We don't go through it, but stay on the west side of the valley, walking down past Huset, "the House", hub of cultural and festive activities in town. More on Huset later.

I reach the quay an hour before we are scheduled to leave, but only just in time for the last tender back to the ship. All of the tourists had already returned from the town centre, and it hadn't occurred to the crew that there might be anyone else on their way back, so they decided to pack up early.

Not long after, we weigh anchor and set course to-wards the mouth of the fjord. At dinner that evening the elegant cruise director and his gracious companion ask me whether I had a good day visiting Longyearbyen. Yes, yes I did, I reply. ▨

We walk to the underground station. We have a day in Oslo before moving on, northwards. It's summer, who needs sleep? "Bring Renata to Nydalen," my friend Eli says over the phone. "It's a new neighbourhood, where urban Oslo has tamed nature, a river bathing place in the city. Just hop on the Circle line and you'll be there in under 15 minutes. We can picnic there, and you can swim off the traveller's grime, sleep an hour or two in the sun."

"The buildings are so grey and brown here," remarks Renata. How did I never notice that? The Oslo of my mind is a colourful place, composed of red farmhouses in the snow, painted wooden suburbia. I hardly ever go to those parts of the city any more, but my childhood lens remains. For each of us, this is a different trip, this book a bridge between our subjectivities. As we write and rewrite our present and my past. Renata's too.

She is Peruvian, but of Japanese origin. It sounds strangely exotic, but in fact there was a wave of Japanese migration to Peru in the early 1900s. Renata's parents never went back, but she decided to learn about her Asian roots and go to Japan to study. Then she got a grant to study in China instead. She ended up studying Cantonese and Chinese painting in Guangzhou and now identifies more than anything with the Chinese diaspora in Peru.

This is part of how we became friends, both of us caught between cultures. And crazy about Cantonese food. We met in a small Chinese restaurant on the rue Saint Jacques in Paris – a cheap place I used to go to when I was a student at the Sorbonne. I was there with friends and heard someone at the next table talking about wanting to exchange art lessons in return for English. I had been looking to improve my drawing skills so I walked over and introduced myself. We only ever did about three sessions, but we've been friends ever since.

But we're not talking about art – or politics – today. The water in the river is cool and we swim against the current like pale salmon. Young women hold writhing naked babies, giggling children splash and play.

Eli, a journalist I know from a former life, is here with her French husband and baby daughter and niece, so we are part of this tableau. Teenagers laugh loudly and drink beer in the sun. Families further up on the grass bring out their disposable barbecues, and I ponder on the strength of a tradition that makes one-use grills so popular in a country otherwise known for a culture of sustainability. For once Renata is too distracted to think about the ecopolitics of the scene. For her this is an anthropological experience and she observes the Norwegians at length, amusing herself by classifying them into different categories, "I can see that there's a Marianne type, and an Eli type, and an Ingrid Bergman type..."

"Hey, Ingrid Bergman was Swedish!"

"I don't care, her type is definitely well represented."

The shadows grow longer and the afternoon stretches out. Time stretches out. Our flight will leave well after midnight. Still time to see Liv at the Opera. Liv is Eli's sister. Whereas Eli is firmly anchored in the world, I think of Liv as a sort of elf, or maybe a *hulder*, a female spirit that hides deep in the woods according to Norwegian folklore. An infinitely gentle but somehow wild woman, slim and wispy haired, familiar with all the plants and herbs and mushrooms that grow in the forest. We got to know each other by staying in each other's homes before we actually met. I remember studying with curiosity the intaglio prints on the wall of her basement studio. That was through Eli who is forever connecting people. Liv works at the Opera part time, and can maybe sneak us in to get a glimpse of a performance from the ushers' booth. Drying off, we change discreetly under our sarongs that serve as towels, wiggling wet swimsuits off and underwear on. No one bothers to watch. Let's go. The Circle line will take us back to the city centre.

The Opera. In winter its buildings rise from the frozen edges of the fjord like sections of sea ice grinding together and pushing up. But today the evening is soft and warm, the deep plush colour of the sky deepening in the east over the white block, a hint of pale gold leaf still

I AM CURIOUS TO
LEARN MORE ABOUT THE
UNDERGROUND ARTISTS'
COLLECTIVE THAT THE
USHERS WORKING FOR
THE OPERA HOUSE
HAVE CREATED.

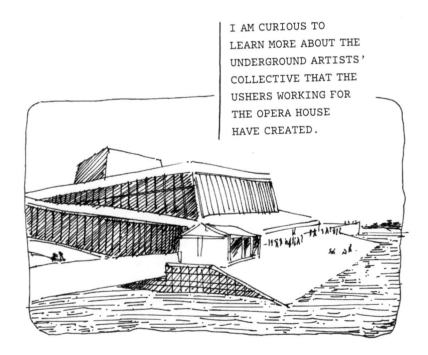

in the west. Liv is waiting outside the main entrance when we arrive. Our voices are muted, the herring gulls' screeches almost drown out the rest – they are fighting for scraps of food down on the water.

"Renata, this is Liv, Eli's sister, also an artist. Liv – Renata. We met in Paris more than 20 years ago. Renata does paintings and line drawings. So I proposed this project to her, based on Aristophanes' play *The Birds*. Our latest idea is a mixed genre graphic novel cum play – a sort of collage – relating a trip through the Arctic."

A letter with enclosures
an illustrated journey through space and time, warped by
strange obsessions
rainbow-looped with innumerable digressions
the expression of the landscape or a face
a snap from the top of an old pole catching a halo
will it hold?

Depending on who I am talking to I explain it differently. I have trouble choosing lenses. Liv nods diplomatically.

And then I tell Renata about Liv, again – because I have already told her about all the people she is going to meet – about Liv's beautiful lithographs and woodcuts, and her mother who lives in a house in the forest in Sweden. I've been there too.

"Nice to meet you," says Liv. "I don't need to start work just yet. If you like we can walk around the outside of the building?" Up the steps on the seaward side, three sets of footsteps echo, an ostinato to the soprano line of the gulls circling above; we are not completely in sync but somehow together.

"Is there anything interesting on tonight?"

The Opera is the perfect location for a fleeting theatrical experience between trains or flights, right next to Oslo S, the central station. It also houses an underground artists' collective that a small group of ushers has created. But Liv, or maybe her friend Maria, can tell you more about that at another time or in another book.

"There's a contemporary play starting this evening. I don't know the company. Actually you might be interested."

"Look," says Renata, pointing to a poster, "It seems to be something about birds."

I shiver and feel my throat do something strange. Is it by Petter? He and I had talked about it a few times. The first time was that night without dark when the two of us sat up late on that trip south. The boat was on autopilot, but I kept an eye on the sea and the coast glowing quietly on the eastern side. I had brought up the parallels I saw between Aristophanes' *The Birds*, the crazy parody of Athenian discontent, and the Arctic microcosm of Longyearbyen. And the birds themselves. Each bird with its distinct place in that peculiar ecosystem. "You should write a play about it," he encouraged, "Why don't you do it?" I replied that he was the one with the experience, and I think we said then that we could write it together.

I haven't seen or spoken to Petter in more than 15 years. I looked for him online a couple of times, but could no longer bring myself to write or call. Nor did I ever ask any of the other friends who I did stay in touch or eventually reconnect with. I just censored myself and stopped looking.

But no, this is not the right story. I am the one re-writing Aristophanes' play. That is what I am doing here. I look at the poster. Based on *Fuglane – The Birds*, a novel by Tarjei Vesaas. The director is someone I have never heard of. I shiver again, but my throat goes back into place. Vesaas's novel is also a tale of an encounter between worlds. But so completely different from what I am trying to do. So different and unreachable that it can only be inspiration.

Renata and I are both sensitive to serendipity. "Isn't this a strange coincidence?" she asks. I wonder if it is the universe nudging me. But to do what or go where? Sometimes the universe seems to be sharing signs but no instructions. I think I am already on a path, but is it veering off course again? Or is it keeping me on track this time?

Renata is familiar with my theory of destiny interchanges, people and places that take your life in a different direction. It may only be a slight deviation from your previous direction at first, but can end up becoming a radical change in the narrative. Maybe she was one of them – or I was for her? Longyearbyen certainly was in its own right. Then there was the Kid of course, and several other people and places I have known.

It's a play based on the novel The Birds, by Tarjei Vesaas - my favourite Norwegian writer.

MARIANNE IS ALWAYS LOOKING OUT FOR (OR GETTING SIDETRACKED BY) SIGNS.

It must be a sign.

Learning to speak (1992)

I ring the doorbell a couple of times, bang on the front door, shouting through the lock, "Rise, worm!" - it is more affectionate than it sounds, a sort of convention between us. The door finally opens; blurred eyes, hoarse voice, he climbs back under his eiderdown as I take my place at the computer and type away at my dissertation on the Norse god Odin. I am in my fourth year at the Sorbonne, struggling through a degree in historical anthropology.

That's how the working day begins. I have biked across Paris, building my would-be Armstrong thighs against the gradient of Belleville in the winter sun. I come here to cook and clean for the Kid. That's part of my brief. More importantly, I answer the telephone - briefly assuming the role of the secretary in the office he doesn't have - in exchange for use of his computer, something I don't have.

You won't hear much more about the Kid in this story but he is important. Without him, none of the rest would have ever happened.

The phone starts ringing. I pick up, "I'm very sorry, Monsieur is not available to answer your call right now - may I take a message?" The Kid stirs under his eiderdown, and we eventually go out for a coffee. We take a seat on the terrace where we order the usual black coffee and a slice of baguette with butter. The shot of caffeine jolts him into life and he starts speaking passionately about publicity, "We've got to get 10 cases in at the Locomotive, it will be our breakthrough. But I still haven't paid for the last 50 cases I ordered for promotional activities... Maybe I can catch up on the smoked salmon front. We're going to have to fight because we're outsiders in this market."

He is talking about the pale Arctic lager that he imports, which Takao (our Osaka-born rock-star-turned-carpenter friend who is studying Old Icelandic with us) calls polar bear pee.

But back to the Kid, who is passionate about what is actually a pleasant boutique beer, and the nightclub scene that he is trying to break into. He's considered small fry, not aligned with any of the major cartels. I sketch as he speaks, using him as model for the main character in my somewhat confidential cartoon series, *The Lonesome Policeman*, circulated only to close friends and loosely inspired by *The Singing Detective*.

We pool our coins to pay, cheeky sparrows darting between our feet to vacuum up the crumbs under the table where we are sitting. He stops to make a long-distance call from the nearby phone booth before we head back to the 20th floor studio apartment that serves as a base. The 1970s buildings that crown this hill on the periphery of Paris have a stunning view, although the neighbourhood itself can be a little dodgy.

I work through the day, pausing only to answer the phone and cook lunch, generally pasta or fried rice, which we eat to a soundtrack from Ennio Morricone's cowboy period.

In the evenings the Kid is brilliant, witty and engaging, with a feverish intelligence forever linking up the ordinary and the extraordinary. He is an extreme extrovert, a sort of alter ego for me, projecting me into places where I would never go alone. He drags me around to cocktail parties, gallery openings, gourmet and cultural events... At one point he is invited to be a guest speaker on cruise ships to Norway - "No, I couldn't do that," he says, "but I wholeheartedly recommend my friend Marianne. She is French-Norwegian, fluent in English as well because she grew up in Australia, and she knows all about Scandinavian history and culture."

So suddenly I am engaged as a lecturer for tourists. I am called to a meeting at the premises of the French Geographical Society where the project is presented to all the new recruits by a weather-beaten Italian explorer and anthropologist, with hundreds of sea miles behind him from Greenland, Svalbard, Iceland and the like. The Anthropologist is a charismatic broad-girthed grizzly-bear type and we are happy and excited to hear him speak of the places we will be travelling to. It transpires that I will be spending the summer on Italian cruise liners sailing up and down the Norwegian coast.

At the beginning of July, I meet the ship in Amsterdam for my first assignment. I want to look professional but my last job was making pancakes for 25 francs an hour in a rundown kebab place and I am desperately impecunious. I turn up in Chinese happy shoes from my local discount store, hoping that they look like casual cruise wear. And begin my new existence, willing myself into this new role. I have a visceral fear of speaking in public, combined with a contradictory drive to do things that I am afraid of, so this is perfect.

And somehow it works out. I find my voice, and the cruise passengers look to me as an authority on any given subject related to Norway. They buy me cocktails and ask my opinion about things. When I get my first pay, I buy new shoes.

The west coast of Norway becomes my beat, and then one day the following year I am asked if I can do the Svalbard cruise. I have heard about this Arctic territory approximately halfway between the north of mainland Norway and the North Pole. It is part of Norway and yet not - anyone from any of the forty-odd nations that have signed the Svalbard Treaty can live and work there freely, providing they abide by Norwegian law, enforced by the local governor.

The name of its main settlement, Longyearbyen, always used to sound like a tyre manufacturer to me, conjuring up an image of burnt rubber in the ice.

But I am also sensitive to the poetry and wilderness of this destination. Of course. ▨

Renata thinks my "destiny interchange" theory might have been inspired by the cult children's classic *The Phantom Tollbooth*. I can't remember whether I even read it as a kid although I do recall I owned a copy – the cover was yellow with a line drawing of a lonely tollbooth attendant and a curious child faced with a spaghetti mess of feeders looped around in a stacked mutant multi-leaved-clover interchange. Is this my life?

Liv leads us into the foyer and past the bar. "Does anyone want a drink?" Renata asks. Nobody does. We walk upstairs and take our seats.

"Have you read the novel?" Liv wonders. "Do you have a particular fascination with birds?" She is a discreet person, but also likes to pry gently to find out what lies under the surface. Our friendship is made up of lots of dots that we are slowly connecting and filling in with pictures from other parts of our lives.

"Yes, I have and Vesaas is one of my favourite writers." He is the master of subjective experience and we agree that his characters have an intense and poignant inner light.

"But to answer your other question, I was not really fascinated by birds until I went to Svalbard," I continue, "Maybe because life there is so constrained. It is the opposite to the tropics where life forms seem to be infinite. Never completely known or knowable. In the Arctic living things are so visible against the emptiness that they seem to become larger than life. In particular the birds. They have strong personalities and many of them will make it clear if they don't want you around."

"So that's why you wanted to write a play about them?" she prods a bit more. I think she finds my project a little hard to grasp.

"No, it's more that I wanted to write about Svalbard, and *The Birds* by Aristophanes seems to fit so well. In the original play two Athenians, fed up with their life in the city, seek out the realm of the birds in the sky. They find it and convince the birds to build a wall around it in order to control and monetize communication between humans and the gods.

"Svalbard is right at the edge of the Arctic ice sheet, far away from the metropolises of Europe and North America, a bit like the far-flung realm of the birds in the play.

"But it is strategically placed between different powers and geopolitical interests, and has represented high stakes at different periods in history. In 1920, the Svalbard Treaty awarded sovereignty over the islands to Norway but gave all signatory countries the right to carry out economic activities in the territory. During World War II, the Germans established weather stations on the islands to collect meteorological data for the war administration. During the Cold War, both Norway and Russia took pains to develop their mining activities and establish communities of people who would live there all year round."

I'm not used to launching into such lengthy expositions. I take a breath.

"So who do you think really owns the place," asks Renata, "Norway? All of the countries that signed? Just the ones that are active there?"

"That's the thing," I ponder, "Maybe none of the above. And there are always private economic interests that come into play as well, whatever the intentions of the governments.

"I want the play to reflect the threat of climate change and the speculation that comes with it, which stretches way beyond Svalbard. So many view the melting of the Arctic as an opportunity. An opportunity that will only further entrench the vicious circle of environmental exploitation in the name of growth.

"Anyway, instead of Aristophanes's comical duo, Pisthetaerus and Euelpides from Athens, I have come up with the characters of Paulsen and Juelsen from southern Scandinavia. They travel up to Svalbard to relax in the cooler climate. And to convince the inhabitants to build a wall and make a business out of climate change. The inhabitants are all birds. I love the personalities of the Arctic birds and I think they are absolutely perfect as the real owners of Svalbard, canny but vulnerable. Anyway, this is what I want to try to write about.

"Back when I was in Svalbard two decades ago, people didn't talk so much about the climate. They did talk about the environment though – like why Norway would even still be mining coal in this one last outpost."

"Yes, it is strange about the mining," says Liv. "But I think they're stopping now, or about to stop. Is that right?"

"Yes, that's what I've read, but it must be a painful social process, because mining is part of the DNA of the community there." Even when I was there, the mining jobs were getting fewer, a tearing apart of the old social fabric.

Renata cuts into my thoughts, "But what's the deal with Norway and fossil fuels anyway? There's the whole oil industry. Nice clean hydro at home while supplying oil to the rest of the world – isn't that a bit ironic?"

It's hard for me to answer. I do know that Norway is also exporting its knowhow in the area of renewables, but sometimes it seems that that is just shouting into the wind.

As for myself, I don't even shout. I whisper at best. No wonder my words float away like little puffs of cloud, stray thought bubbles. I'm not an activist. I like to think it's because I always see both sides of the story, but maybe I'm just lacking in conviction. Maybe I'm just afraid. Always afraid.

The lights in the theatre dim and we stop talking.

We are at the back of the main concert hall, high up in the gods, holding the binoculars that Liv has lent us. As the play begins it strikes me that sitting quietly here as we crane to see what is happening through these tiny lenses is like bird-watching.

Outdoors again now. We praise the play and pick apart the direct-ing, just a bit, as people wander off in different directions, to catch trains, find their car, grab a bite to eat. Some, mostly young people, linger on the slope that leads down to the water, together with people who have been there all evening, talking, smoking joints. One small group has a guitar. At an earlier point in my life, they would have been my tribe. Now I am not sure who my tribe is.

"How long does it usually take to check in?" Renata asks. I am the trip organizer, but she is keeping tabs, she knows I can get distracted and veer off course, even without any particularly destiny-changing event. I check my phone – we'd better get to the airport.

The moon is hanging low over the runway and I think I spot the silhouette of a lone kestrel gliding in the distance as we take off. And now we are flying back into the dawn. The day... The day that lasts forever... I nod off.

MARIANNE

MARIANNE

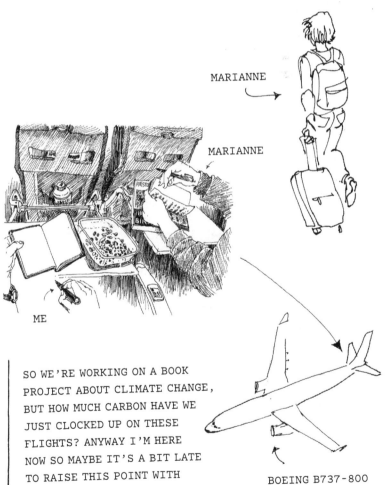

ME

SO WE'RE WORKING ON A BOOK
PROJECT ABOUT CLIMATE CHANGE,
BUT HOW MUCH CARBON HAVE WE
JUST CLOCKED UP ON THESE
FLIGHTS? ANYWAY I'M HERE
NOW SO MAYBE IT'S A BIT LATE
TO RAISE THIS POINT WITH
MARIANNE...

BOEING B737-800

Day 1
Flight forward

I must have fallen asleep. I wake at around 3.30 a.m. to a change in the cabin light. Are those clouds or mountains below us? White peaks like whipped egg whites.

My heart beats faster – Rosendo, I'm scared. Sorry, I mean Renata, or do I mean Auden? I forgot I was supposed to be inside the story. But even inside I am still scared and not quite sure who I am talking to. How are the days ahead going to unfold?

I always tell people that life gets better as you get older. It gets easier. You get over the complexes. But in the end maybe it's just the building up of a protective shell after all. A process of adding on rather than shedding. And now those layers of self-assurance that I have built up over the years seem to be falling away.

I have left my two daughters with my mother in Paris and told them that I won't be in touch for a week. They're used to this – it's my modus operandi when I go on assignments for work. Another kind of shedding. A stripping away of the people who make me one kind of person. So I can be the person underneath again. Or just someone else.

But this time it is different. My job with the magazine makes me feel grown-up – it's real and people pay me for it. I have to respect word limits and deadlines and I have developed a set of techniques for putting together an article. But now I am here for me, another someone else again – and if it weren't for Renata I would be adrift.

I feel guilty about Renata as well. I have dragged her into this project, sold her on the collaboration, but it's going to be hard to keep my end of the deal. She is completely different to me – they say artists are disconnected from reality, have their head in the clouds. But she has an iron-willed sense of discipline and responsibility. Her trust in me is the trust of a true friend – she knows that there is something inherently flaky about me, but she is willing to take the chance. Make that wager.

The plane starts to descend.

The first time I touched down at this airport, it was also summer, and around the same time of day. It was about a year after my first brief visit, when I had arrived on the cruise ship. I had been swimming that day too; not in the city but out in Nordmarka, the woods that surround the city of Oslo, basking in the earthy smell where forest meets lake in the sun.

ACCORDING TO THE BROCHURE I AM READING, A GUIDE CAN
TAKE US TO THE TOP OF A SUMMIT SURROUNDED BY UNTOUCHED
NATURE. UNTOUCHED? WHAT ABOUT ALL THE TOURISTS WHO
HAVE ALREADY BEEN UP THERE? COME AND SOIL THIS NUBILE
PEAK BEFORE SOMEONE DECIDES TO PROTECT IT? THERE GOES
MY WICKED TONGUE AGAIN. ANOTHER ARGUMENT WITH MARIANNE
COMING UP…

Arrival by air (1994)

It is 3 a.m. Daylight, but although the sun will not set for another couple of months it is nowhere to be seen. The sky has been dimmed out by a curtain of grey-lit snowflakes, and the pilot has announced an outside temperature of 3°C. I have arrived with some mountain gear, a pair of rubber boots, a box of books and 1000 kroner in my pocket.

There was supposed to be someone here to meet me.

I enquire at the information desk as the other passengers disperse. Groups gather their luggage and depart on a bus. Individual travellers spot their names on signs held by rugged-looking men and women who whisk them away in four-wheel drives. "Maybe you should talk to one of the tour operators," the lady at the information desk suggests, pointing me in the direction of a stocky ginger-haired German. We introduce ourselves and I realize I know his name – "Oh, aren't you the author of that guide to Spitzbergen?" A book I'd come across in a little bookstore in Hunter Street, Sydney, a couple of years back. He is.

The German has no idea about me or my situation, but is friendly and offers to help. He can at least drive me

into town. We climb into his beaten-up old orange van
that stands out against the soft grey landscape like
forgotten orange peel in the snow. We talk about the
Arctic and travels and tourists.

Is tourism damaging the fragile Arctic environment?

"Not if it's done in the right way. It's more sustainable than mining."

By the time we get into town and I have told him more
about my story he offers me a place to sleep for the night.
It's not a hook-up plan - just a kind gesture that ties in
with the culture of this small community perched at the
edge. He gives me the keys to an empty studio apartment that
is awaiting his next batch of guides, and promises to take
me the next morning to the office that manages apartment
rentals. I am immensely grateful, especially as the only
hotel in town costs 400 kroner a night.

The cliff opposite the studio block is teeming with
little auks, small black-and-white birds whose upright
demeanour makes them look a bit like fairy penguins.
Despite their incessant chattering, I manage to get a
few hours' sleep, tossing and turning on the sofa bed in
the grey daylight.

At a certain point the brightest part of the grey
seems to have switched sides, which tells me that it must
be morning. I climb into the fluorescent orange van when
the kind ginger-haired German comes to pick me up to take
me to the rental agency. Perhaps an apartment has been
booked for me, and even if not, renting a flat has to be
cheaper than the hotel - I would only be able to afford
two nights there (providing I don't eat), or perhaps a
little more if I manage to sell all the books in the box I
brought with me. I imagine myself setting up shop in the

port to catch the cruise ship arrivals like the Icelandic music student.

It is a 2-minute ride down to the centre of town, which consists of a multi-purpose store, a self-service cafeteria, a bank and a couple of other small buildings. Rifles are propped up outside the doors of the various buildings - guns are part of the culture here but you can't take them inside. You do have to have one if you go beyond the town centre though. Shortly before I arrived this summer, a young woman walking over the plateau was taken by a bear, and the town is still recovering from the tragedy. That very plateau I had sauntered across alone and gunless in my Doc Martens the year before.

This year I have a fixed ticket with a return in one month's time, so I had better come up with a plan. Perhaps the German knows of someone who might need a French-speaking guide?

"Yes, I do, you should meet him," he says.

"Oh, actually, there he is," he adds, pointing to a blue-eyed man with tangled blond hair pulling up in the car next to us. It is the blond latter-day Viking I had met on the mountain the year before. Same red-checked shirt even.

"Hi there, I remember you. You're the girl from the cruise ships. How was your walk up Nordenskiöldtoppen last summer?"

Do they need French-speaking guides? "Yes, maybe, look me up one of these days - first office on the left in Nybyen."

The rental service informs me that an apartment has in fact been booked for me. This is a relief. At least I'll be able to live somewhere, if not eat. My apartment is in the same block as the ginger-haired German and his guides, on the east side, in road 222. They are a mixed crowd of Germans, English and Swedes who I will quickly get to know.

We are just up the hill from the town centre, in the middle of one of the rows of multicoloured houses that contrast sharply with the dark mouths of the old mine entrances. Colour is taken seriously here. A specially appointed architect decides upon the shade and tone of any new construction so that it will fit in harmoniously with the rest of the structures nestled along the shoulders of the treeless valley.

The sugarloaf hillside above the rows of houses is a bit unstable and will be threatened by avalanches years later, possibly linked to changing weather patterns and warmer temperatures. Its residents will be permanently evacuated. But I don't know that yet. For now, it feels like home.

I try to call the man who has sent me up here. The Italian Anthropologist not only writes and lectures on cruise ships, he also has an entrepreneurial bent and wants me to help set up a guiding service for cruise tourists in Longyearbyen. I ring his number numerous times but cannot get through. I try the Kid too, he is someone who knows everyone and can solve anything - but he is not answering either, maybe his new secretary is not in the office yet. Next stop, Svalbardbutikken, the store, where the Anthropologist told me an office will be waiting for me that I can use to run the guiding operations. I walk into the place where you can get everything from vegetables to wine to polar bear souvenir mugs and puffin t-shirts.

"Who?" asks the store manager, a tall and dark bear-like fellow with a wide face and friendly smile. He doesn't seem to know what I am talking about, at least at first. And then, "Actually, that does ring a bell, there was someone in here last year who mentioned a project like yours in passing. I think he was Italian. But we never heard from him again."

Amazingly, Bear and his colleague, a man who looks like a character from an Ibsen play, agree to help me as long as I can help them out in turn with some transla-tions they need done. They set me up in an office with a computer and telephone and over the following days I try to organize something to make this guiding service happen. But there is no company structure, no insur-ance, no way of setting up a bank account and I don't have the strength, or the will, or the knowledge, to do everything from A to Z.

In the meantime I start working on the translations and format little signs for the shop to sell coffee mugs and postcards. I even manage to broaden my clientele, which now includes the Museum, where I end up translat-ing into English and French the signage and little notes that accompany the exhibits. Maybe my translated notes are still there?

Ibsen adopts me and becomes my self-appointed guide to the settlement that summer. His melancholy face, framed by a long thin beard and sideburns, lights up with a smile when I arrive for work in the mornings. He plies me with gallons of weak coffee and introduces me to lunches at the Busen café, meatballs, fishballs and the like. He lends me a bicycle, a CD player and some music, and welcomes me into his circle of friends.

The German and I also become friends, and his guides my walking companions. Whenever we have a spare moment and the weather is good we explore the environs, whatever time of day or night it might be. There is Pixie, an energetic redhead with wicked green eyes, the quiet and thoughtful Geologist from England, the Gentle Giant from Germany who had unsuccessfully tried to halt his growth spurt by going vegetarian, and the Artist, who becomes a good friend for a while and who I will even meet up with in France a few years later.

The Artist and his friends will roll up in Paris in a car packed with rucksacks and sleeping bags and pick me up on a street corner. They take me to a crazy party in a country town on a night of shooting stars, but somehow I don't feel right and leave early next morning without waking anyone to catch the early train back home. I am still not quite sure why I am struck by social anxiety just then – but it is partly to do with feeling like a misfit and partly to do with Petter and my dilemmas of the heart at that time. Yet I used to love talking to the Artist about art and the Arctic and performance and life pathways. I google him many years later and discover he has participated in an exhibition in the only art gallery in the street I am living in in Paris. Which I somehow completely missed. A case of paths crossing but not intersecting.

The German wonders how I'm going with my guiding initiative and translation work. He needs someone to help out with a project, but can't really pay. I'm game. Plus I'm going nowhere with the guiding.

And so I become sound assistant and general girl Friday for a couple from Berlin who make documentaries in their spare time. They take me further and further away from Longyearbyen, exploring Isfjord by Zodiac. I hold the microphone with utmost care as we capture the sound of young guillemots on a bird cliff or a stream breaking through a glacier.

And beyond, now by helicopter, northwards, soaring like storm petrels across alluvial plains that shine in the afternoon sun, jumping ridges and following glaciers that look like abandoned highways grinding their way down broad valleys. And it seems limitless, and like I will always be able to flee forwards into the daylight. This must be some kind of fairy tale and I'm not sure real life will ever catch up again. ∎

OUR HOSTEL IN NYBYEN LOOKS A BIT
AUSTERE. APPARENTLY THESE WERE
THE BARRACKS WHERE THE MINERS
USED TO LIVE. I WONDER WHETHER
THERE IS A FRIDGE WHERE I CAN
KEEP MY EYEDROPS?

The airport runway is still in the same place, but the building has changed. Among the faces of the tour guides waiting, I recognize no one. Some German tourists turn to us with questions. There is something both poetic and reassuring for me that despite more than 15 years of absence, I am the one answering the newcomers' questions.

And then we are in the bus, hurtling along the road, raising dust as we pass the campsite where the Arctic terns always used to dive-bomb me when I was running errands on my bicycle.

When we get closer to town, I am intimidated by the urban sprawl. I am not the only one who has changed over the years I have been away. Whole neighbourhoods have mushroomed. Nature's edge is receding.

The bus takes us to Nybyen, up towards the top of the valley, on the Lars glacier side. I recognize the old miners' quarters. At least this area doesn't seem to have changed so much since I was here last, although there are more tourists and fewer locals. And among the locals, many seem to be Thai. In fact, I discover, there are now more Thais in Longyearbyen than any other nationality except Norwegians. This is an unexpected development – as are the Thai restaurants and food stores. It seems bizarre to me – a culture I associate with the tropics transplanted here, one of the northernmost settlements on earth. But then I realize that the Thais are no more incongruous than the Norwegians. We are all clinging to our fragile humanity in the face of nature.

We are in a hostel a couple of buildings up from the one I used to work in, and more or less opposite another one I lived in for a while. It is moot whether to treat this arrival time as the end of the night or the beginning of the next morning – by this time it is about 5 a.m. – but I reckon this is Day 1. A friendly young woman checks us in. "I'm Janike from Sweden," she says, "Welcome to Longyearbyen."

There are four of us in the room, and we are an eclectic bunch where any given two people have a specific language combination: I usually speak French with Renata, but Jon – the Swedish Finn – speaks Spanish, so that's his preferred language when talking to her. I speak to

him in Norwegian and to Kevin the British Hong Konger in English, whereas Renata and Kevin speak Cantonese together. Again my preference for second-class travel and my budget coincide – it's easier to meet people when you travel on a shoestring.

Kevin looks like a quintessential city-dweller with a quirky haircut, but it turns out he is a solitary soul who chases eclipses and meteorological phenomena around the world. Jon is a photographer by predilection and coder by trade. He has a plump baby face and a warm smile that lights up his brown eyes. He is more gregarious than Kevin and we end up spending a lot of time with him. Starting with now, out on our first urban reconnaissance, philosophizing as we loop around the town, following the main road.

We walk over the river towards Huset first – the House. Huset is, or at least used to be – and tonight it certainly seems like it still is – the cultural and social hub of the town, despite its location at the top of the valley. People eat there, get drunk, dance to Northern Norwegian country music, congregate and hook up. Tonight, the whole building is vibrating with the sound of a massive party that is still in full swing, and the occasional drunken Viking spills out into the daylight. We debate whether to go in – it might be our only chance to experience a true Longyearbyen party. But somehow we can't quite drum up the right mood out of the Arctic zen groove we are just getting into, so we keep walking and the thunder and booms slowly dissipate as we approach the centre of town, where everything is completely still.

"So you're a photographer?" asks Renata, and Jon stops briefly to show her some of the shots he has stored in his camera.

"But let's keep walking," he says. "Photography is my passion, but ultimately also dissatisfying. How can I capture the quality of the light and the special transparency of the air here?" He looks out at the fjord and the sky and the bare mountains.

"But you don't have to capture it, or demand satisfaction," replies Renata. "Isn't it a dialogue?

"We are all just interpreting reality. It's not ours to capture, we can't own it. If anything, we are captured within it."

Jon is taken aback by her tone, but I recognize Renata's way of challenging someone through their choice of words. She is always very precise, and loves sparring with her conversation partners.

"You're right," he replies, "but I always want to come closer to the essence. I guess that's what I mean, to remove the layers that get in the way of seeing clearly."

I'm not sure I agree. Doesn't he see that those layers are part of our reality? That the layers that we capture and express are what define us, just as the masks we choose to present ourselves to others ultimately define us.

But I understand better when he compares it to how he feels when he is coding – the paring back of something to its simplest, most elegant form, as something that brings you closer to the truth.

Jon is curious to hear more about the book that we are working on. And I wonder about this writer mask that I am using for myself on this trip. Does it really define me? And will I ever manage to figure out whether I am adding or shedding layers?

We climb into our bunks at about 6 a.m., and are rocked to sleep by rumbling noises coming from Kevin. We wake a few hours later when he rustles up a storm with his windbreaker and other outdoor gear before going out, and then sink back into oblivion until around midday.

We are in luck and breakfast is not quite packed up yet. I introduce Renata to the delights of Norwegian brown cheese ("Kind of like dulce de leche, I'm sure you'll like it, just don't think of it as cheese…") on thick slices of wholemeal bread, and then we go downstairs to pick up the bicycles that are being loaned to us by Tom the Bike, the brother of Tall Viking, who I worked for as a guide all those years ago. He is a younger lighter-haired version of his brother, and a bit more shy. He will be a discreet guardian angel during our stay, and is also going to help us get hold of a gun. The rule has been drilled into me, into every-

one who comes to this place: In Longyearbyen you can't go outside the town limits without a gun. A polar bear can appear at any time.

The bikes are a bit dusty and have flat tires when he gets them out, but Tom the Bike insists on sprucing them up himself. "No, we can do it!" we insist. No, he will. He gets out his tools. I try to make myself useful by holding the bike straight for him, but really I'm mostly just in the way. Renata pulls out her notepad and draws him at work. We talk about Latin America where he travelled for six months, and he relates his unfortunate experiences of feeling squeezed when surrounded by masses of people. He comes back to this image of being squeezed again and again, "I usually try to avoid these kinds of situations."

"Doesn't it ever happen here?" I ask, realizing as I do that it is probably a stupid question. But he ponders, "Well, yes, it does I guess, but in Svalbard it might only happen occasionally in one of the bars."

What is the relationship of space to human contact? Tom wants to avoid feeling squeezed. Kevin is also averse to feeling squeezed, the reason he left Hong Kong, "Too many people". Jon however likes the fact that in Svalbard he meets people. Perhaps together they exemplify the paradox of this place. Longyearbyen is a magnet for scientists, artists, curious travellers and explorers – and the town's population has doubled since I was here in the nineties. Now there are even housing shortages and people sometimes have to cram into friends' living rooms when there are weather emergencies.

Tom the Bike tells us he can't get us a gun just yet, but there seems to be a consensus that we should be fine on our bicycles without one as long as we stick to the road.

We follow the road out towards the mouth of Adventfjord, a small arm of the broad swathe of water – Isfjord – that cuts right through the heart of Spitsbergen, the main island of the Svalbard archipelago. A sign at the side of the road stops us temporarily. "No walking in this area!" Perhaps we should not continue? A large grey car slows down to turn and I ask the blonde woman at the wheel, who reassures me,

SHOOTING PRACTICE ON THE BEACH.
THEY START YOUNG HERE.

"No, don't worry, there's some research going on in the tundra area but you're fine if you stick to the road."

Before she revs up again, I ask her about Hiawatha the trapper, an old friend of mine who I have lost touch with. I had heard he had decided to give up his life as a trapper, and was living down here somewhere now.

"Oh yes, he's back there," she explains, "in a big green house near the crane. He built it himself."

And I think of the character in Leonard Cohen's *Famous Blue Raincoat* who is building a house deep in the desert – or on an island as sung in Norwegian by Kari Bremnes back in '94. Except here he has come back from the island.

"Do you know if he's around?"

"Well, I had dinner with him the other day, so I think he's in town." We take note for the return trip and continue out towards the airport. We pass the entrance to the Global Seed Vault, which houses over a million seeds in tunnels that go deep into the permafrost in case agriculture needs to be kick-started at some point in the future. I recall the first seed bank, created by Norway in the empty shafts of Mine 3, where I used to take visitors while working as a guide.

We stop at the lighthouse near the airport and sit facing out into Isfjord for a while. On our way back, the chain on the bicycle comes loose, and Renata has to develop a new riding technique, kind of like scootering: cruising with one leg and kicking with the other. It occurs to me that we might not be well-placed for a getaway if a bear did come along. I put that thought quietly away. Taking advantage of our slow progress, it is the terns instead who descend upon us near the camping site.

It seems as though nothing has changed from when I used to ride out on my bicycle to drop off gear for some of the campers. There was a particular spot where I would hear a raucous screech signalling that they were about to descend and I should pick up speed. Ultra-

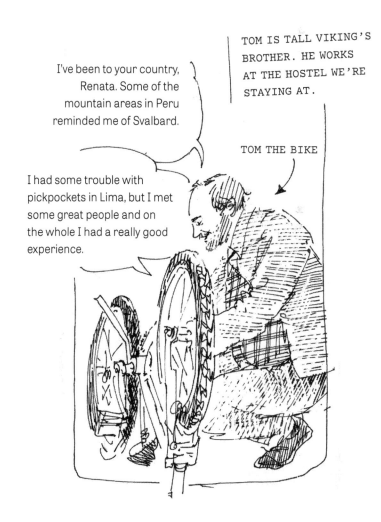

I've been to your country, Renata. Some of the mountain areas in Peru reminded me of Svalbard.

I had some trouble with pickpockets in Lima, but I met some great people and on the whole I had a really good experience.

TOM IS TALL VIKING'S BROTHER. HE WORKS AT THE HOSTEL WE'RE STAYING AT.

TOM THE BIKE

WE'RE NOT FAR FROM TOWN BUT IT FEELS LIKE
THE ENDS OF THE EARTH. I GUESS THERE IS GOOD
VISIBILITY IF A BEAR SHOULD HAPPEN TO TURN
UP BUT WOULD WE BE ABLE TO CYCLE FASTER THAN
A BEAR CAN RUN?

protective of their eggs and offspring, these birds will swoop on any-thing that moves in the vicinity, pecking at people's scalps, sometimes drawing blood. I was an endless source of amusement for the tourists at the campsite as I tried to keep my balance while accelerating up the rise that led past the nesting area, holding an arm over my head as the rifle slung across my back slapped back and forth.

But today we manage to power through without mishap and take a left at the next fork. And then I see a sign I recognize. From the Auckland Port Authority. A sign I last saw when it was still hanging on the annex to Hiawatha the trapper's cabin in Bellsund. As I looked back at the shore before I turned around to look ahead again. But that was my second and last time in Bellsund. For now let me tell you about the first visit.

Sailing south (1995)

My first time to Bellsund. A year before the trip down
with the Skipper and Saskia and Hiawatha and Petter. I
have hitched a ride back to the mainland on the French
yacht as it finishes its summer season in Svalbard.

Bellsund is on the way south, a good place to stop for
anyone sailing back towards mainland Norway. Axelöya,
the island that lies at the junction of the sound and
the deep Van Mijenfjord behind, is home to Hiawatha
the trapper. The Longyearbyen Australian, stock market golden boy turned local field expert, has told us
we could stop by there, "Tell him I sent you," he says.
"Tell him I say hello."

The trapper's cabin is built from driftwood. If
you look carefully, you can see that the wood has been
aligned carefully in a graduation of shades. A rack for
drying seal flesh stands a few metres away.

It looks like no one is home today.

Then the shutters of an upstairs window are flung
open, "I'm on sick leave." Sick leave? It doesn't look
like he wants to socialize. The Golden Boy's name is our
visiting card. It must be a valid reference, as a few

moments later the front door opens and we are invited in for coffee. We sit on weathered whale vertebrae, found along the shore like the driftwood and slotted together as seats. The house has been perfectly designed and fitted together piece by piece. It is a work of fine craftsmanship, a work of art really.

He is suffering from sciatica, but ends up telling us his polar bear stories, like the time he was stuck in -26°C up on the tall wooden frame he uses for drying meat, with a bear circling round at the base, waiting for some live bait.

But no, hang on, this account is not quite accurate. When I found my diaries I saw I had recorded the encounter quite differently. Hiawatha smiles as he opens his window and invites me in before the others. "Can't you keep still?" he asks me when I tell him about my travels.

When we say goodbye I give him a friendly hug. "It was nice to meet you," I say. "I guess it could have been," he replies. I start responding but change my mind.

Hiawatha, who came to Svalbard from the Faroes via Iceland and Greenland and who later became a friend and critic. Who would read my Norwegian poetry and correct the grammar. In his cabin he used to read novels in five or six language versions to compare and critique the translations. Hiawatha, who I last saw one drizzly 17th of May years ago in Tromsø.

Hiawatha has friends who come to help him towards the end of the summer to gather down from the nests of eider ducks, left empty after their yearly migration southwards. Down grows between the skin and the feathers of eider ducks and has a unique soft fluffiness - the ducks use their own down to insulate their nests and keep their

eggs warm. It is perfect for making eiderdowns and col-
lecting the leftover down is a longstanding tradition in
Norway and Iceland. I was to come and help him collect
down one summer. But it never came to be. ▨

This time there appear to be more obvious signs of life at first glance. There are keys in the door and a car is parked outside. I knock. No answer. I knock at the other door – no answer. "Hei!" I call out.

Renata and I debate whether he might be here. Perhaps sleeping? We decide to wait a while and we chat as we eat a snack on the steps in the lee of the wind. The sun is warm on our faces.

"Is it a national trait?" Renata asks, "This brisk greeting? This emphatic 'Hei'?"

"Hmm, I've never thought about it. Perhaps it is the nature of the word itself. The H that requires emphasis to be heard, to open that one solitary diphthong that would otherwise be lost in the wind. It is not like 'Bonjour' which can be eaten up and squeezed through the lips in a mumble, bjr…"

I knock again on both doors, and call out "Hei" once more, so loudly that we both giggle with what might be embarrassment if it turns out that someone can actually hear us. No answer. Perhaps we should go. I tuck a note in between two beams. As we ride away, I look back, wondering whether one of these windows might burst open like so many years ago. But they remain blank.

I can already feel tiredness in my untrained legs as we cycle up towards our temporary home. There is a plump reindeer grazing placidly out front of the first building on the east side of Nybyen, outlined against a pile of black coal – Renata stops to take a photograph. I sit for a moment on the stairs leading up to Block 1 where I used to work.

Cut to Huset. Early evening, for what words like "evening" are worth in this time of no darkness.

We are sitting around the table, Renata, Jon and I. It's quieter today, no trace of last night's earth-shaking vibrations. I look around and it seems so different from how I remember. It has gone upmarket, as my mother would say, lost some of its character. But not all. The curtains are drawn and the candles are lit, as before, sustaining the illusion of a difference between night and day.

SVALBARD
REINDEER

WE SPOTTED THIS FELLOW JUST
OUTSIDE THE HOSTEL. LATER
WE WONDERED WHETHER HE WAS
RELATED TO THE FINNBIFF WE
HAD FOR DINNER AT HUSET.

I am writing, Jon is going through his photographs, Renata is drawing... In fact she is the one who calls out the magic of the place. People are drawn to her and her sketchbook like a magnet. She holds it up to them like a mirror, sketches that capture their quirks and expressions, snippets of conversation captured in speech bubbles – although I'm not quite sure they see *her*, she sort of hides underneath.

"Can you find the odd one out?" she asks as she holds up a page full of stolen portraits, including her own, a thin face with a wide grin.

"What are you writing about?" Jon asks me. He keeps asking me about the book. "I think I'm writing about being an impostor," I reply. "Or maybe I just am an impostor. I'm writing about Svalbard, but I don't really have the credentials to do that. I'm neither an expert nor a local nor a writer. So I came up with the idea of adapting someone else's work, using it as a lens – are you familiar with Aristophanes' *The Birds*?"

He isn't, so I explain the tale of the two Athenians who, fed up with city life and tired of paying taxes, leave Athens to seek out the birds.

"And the birds of Svalbard captivate me, more than any others, I'm not sure why. They are just as quirky and distinctive as the hoopoe and his companions in the play."

"Maybe it's because they really are sovereign here," replies Jon. "And so impressively adapted to this environment. Like the terns. I certainly won't forget coming face to face with those sleek and aggressive birds who defend their nests with beak and claw. And can you believe they fly all the way from here to Antarctica and back each year?"

"Yes, my Uncle Otto used to say my mother was like a tern, flying back and forth between Australia and Norway throughout her life."

"She had a sharp tongue too," adds Renata, a little wickedly.

Jon has scrolled through to some bird photos and invites us to have a look. Plump snow ptarmigans captured as they potter about on the slopes, sandpipers skittering along the beach.

"Anyway," I go on, "the characters in my play are climate profiteers who decide to set their sights northwards. These people exist. When

MARIANNE TELLS ME THAT NORWAY IS BECOMING MORE AND MORE MULTI-ETHNIC BUT I'M DEFINITELY THE ODD ONE OUT HERE AT HUSET THIS EVENING.

the crunch comes the quick and the clever will escape the heat. And the big investors will turn towards the resources being uncovered by the melting ice. Not to mention the shipping routes that are opening up. It's already happening."

"Yeah, Scandinavia is already filling up with data centres," Jon adds, "The company I work for manages several." He looks pensive and I feel uncomfortable. I don't want to make him feel guilty. Or do I?

"Will you read it when I'm done?" I ask.

"Of course," he reassures me, and we all retreat to our respective inner worlds as we wait for our dinner orders to arrive.

A lanky waitress arrives with three large plates balanced along one arm. We have all ordered the day's special, *finnbiff*, a northern Norwegian preparation of reindeer meat. Savours of crushed juniper, sharp lingonberries, sweet brown cheese and game. Is it Svalbard reindeer that we are eating – maybe a relative of the one we saw earlier? Probably not, I suppose. I know that even authorized residents are allowed to cull a maximum of one per year, which is why the reindeer tend to wander so nonchalantly around the settlements.

It's only about 7 p.m. but Renata and I are fading and decide to head back over to our side of the valley. Who cares about the time in this place where day shades into more day? We can just go to bed. Jon stays on at Huset – he's meeting some other new friends for a drink.

Not quite sure if this is an afternoon nap or bed for the night, but both Renata and I wake later at about 10 p.m. I check my phone and see there are two messages. The first from my Uncle Otto, "Will you please join us for dinner at Uncle Bjørn's when you are back in Oslo next week?"

Uncle Otto is one of my heroes. He spent many years living in Greenland, starting as a trapper back in the 1950s and ending up as guardian of the Northeast Greenland National Park, the largest national park in the world and about one and a half times the size of the whole of France. Before he moved to Greenland he had wanted to be a painter.

SOMETIMES WE HAVE TO RETREAT
INTO OUR OWN WORLDS.

My father told me they walked all over Oslo together in the summer of 1951 looking for a pair of corduroy trousers because he was going to move to Paris to become an artist. And that is what artists wore. But an offer came up to become a trapper instead. Confirmation came in the form of a phone call in the spring of 1952. "Can you ski?" Yes. "Do you have a gun?" No. "Don't worry, we can get you one. There's an opening for a trapper if you're still interested." He climbed on a boat and spent his first of many winters in Kap Herschell in north-eastern Greenland.

He never gave up his painting though. His landscapes, infused with light. He even made a portrait of my mother in sad haunting tones of mustard and green.

And the second message on my phone: "Knock harder next time – was that you on the bicycles?"

I call back, "Hiawatha, hello, so good to hear your voice! Did you read our note? When can we see you?"

We will go back down and visit Hiawatha a bit later – he's going fishing now, but any time between 2 and 4 a.m. would be fine. It is only our first day here but this kind of timing already seems completely normal, even to Renata.

Day 2
Fossils

We bike back down to see Hiawatha at 2 a.m., but we don't find him at home and the keys aren't in his door this time. So we scout along the shore where he said he had planned to go fishing.

I see two men out by some sheds but don't recognize either of them. I walk towards them to ask if they have seen Hiawatha, but they seem focused on what they are doing, standing together without a word. I feel like I am intruding and start beating a retreat back behind the sheds along the waterfront. But when I see that they are packing up their gear and coming in my direction, I pluck up my courage and start walking back towards them. "Marianne!" one of them calls out. Oh, so it is him, the taller of the two, but he is so much thinner now that I didn't recognize his silhouette from a distance. His hair is greyer too, although his eyes seem brighter than before. Or perhaps his more angular face brings them into relief. He must be in his early sixties now, I think – last time I saw him he was in his forties. And I was in my twenties. The intervening years have marked us both.

He gives me a warm hug. "Renata," I turn and call, "come and meet Hiawatha!" She joins us and we all exchange greetings. The younger man says goodbye almost immediately after, and Renata, Hiawatha and I wheel our bicycles back towards the big green house where Hiawatha now lives.

I am happy to see him. A cranky and sometimes cruel friend, he is also generous and gifted with a keen intelligence. Not only knowledgeable about animals, winds, tides, seasons, killing and nurturing – already a universe in itself – but also capable of building a house, setting up complex alternative energy systems, navigating, working heavy machinery. An inventor. A linguist with a perfect command of Norwegian and excellent command of English, widely read and insightful about the world at large, well beyond his corner of the Arctic.

Happy to see him, too, because since I began this trip he is my first link with before, reconnecting me to my previous self, the little pieces of myself that belonged here two decades ago.

"Have a look at these photos. I had a great sixtieth birthday party! Huset did the catering, they even brought all the cutlery."

"Oh, but you didn't invite me," I needle him, not expecting that he should have. We haven't been in touch for years.

"No, I only invited people who deserved it. I invited everyone who ever came and helped me to collect down from the eider nests on Axeløya. But you never came."

I refrain from reminding him that he was the one who asked me not to come in the end, and look more closely at the photo. I recognize Petter's asymmetrical face and ropy dark hair from among the guests clustered around the table. I guess their friendship was different.

Renata has gone to the bathroom and there is a moment of silence.

"I am sorry though," he continues, "about that letter I wrote back then, criticizing your Norwegian translations. I was awake nights on end agonizing over it… Don't get me wrong, my criticism was justified, but I regret the way I said it."

"Oh, you remember that?" I look over at him in surprise. I had forgotten. More accurately, I had put it out of my mind, that letter where he put me down, criticizing my presumptuousness in wanting to be a translator, cutting to the core of my issues with identity. My French is not flawless either – I am a third culture kid who grew up in several countries. But I can write a decent article and my editor knows my limitations – I'm not seen as a native speaker so there's not that pressure to be absolutely perfect.

I guess that was when I stopped writing to him. So if I think about it, it is not the event forgotten in the mists of time that I told myself it was, surprised that he would even bring it up. Quite the opposite. It is where we left off. And he is picking back up from there now. Now that we are seeing each other again for the first time in years. He has a cruel side, it is true, but he is more honest and perspicacious than I am.

His warm-cold friendship continues today. "Why didn't you come and stay with me instead of staying in town?" he asks at one point. "You are welcome here." But later when we leave and I suggest meeting again, he replies "maybe".

"Remember that play I wanted to write?" I ask him. "The one you helped me try to get funding for?" The one I didn't ever get any funding for. I wasn't together enough. I hadn't written enough. And I didn't have enough knowledge about communication. Enough capacity for spin.

"Yes, why?"

"I'm finally writing it. Would you be willing to read it, comment on it?" I know he would tear it to pieces, but I could do with that.

"Are you sure you want me to?" he asks, and offers me a glass of aquavit. I think he wants to avoid hurting my feelings again. He is more sensitive about it than he might have been in the past.

We are sipping the Linie aquavit quietly when Renata returns. "So I guess you've told Hiawatha about the book we're working on?" she comments.

"Well, not exactly. Just the play aspect."

"You have to tell him!" But it is she who continues, in a mix of rusty English and her native Spanish, which Hiawatha understands a little. "It's a sort of graphic novel," she says, looking mainly at Hiawatha now as he pours a glass for her, "combined with a play. Do you mind if we

put you in it? We might change your character a bit of course."

"In that case, yes, I would like to review it," he notes. "By the way, did you know that this aquavit is stored on a cargo ship to age as it circumnavigates the globe?"

"Yes, it's the one my father used to drink. He was a captain and sailed around the world a number of times himself," I comment and we raise a toast.

Renata doesn't only want to sketch, she also wants some photos. We pose awkwardly, but she catches the softness of a mitten of knitted musk ox wool being passed between us. Hiawatha brings out a ball of eider down from the nests around his island home. So soft too. I restrain myself from asking for a small tuft, and we discuss the virtues of Indian cotton versus Chinese cotton for eiderdown covers (the latter rustles more).

He shows us photos. Of the orphaned eider chicks that he had to stuff into his pockets to take home and keep warm when their parents had been taken by polar bears. They cheeped so much when he left them in a box that he took them out again and let them settle around his chest and beard and then they quietened down.

He tells us about the bears that have been coming more and more often and try to cull the birds and take their eggs.

"Do you think it's climate change?" I ask. "Or have you may- be changed the ecosystem by protecting the birds?" He's not sure. Everything is connected.

At around 3:30 a.m. we climb back on our bicycles.

Jon is still out when we arrive. When he gets in around breakfast time he tells us about his adventures and apologizes for smelling like alcohol... He got caught up in his first true Longyearbyen party.

The Longyearbyen parties were an institution. Almost a ritual. There is the *forspill* or before-party, to get slightly drunk beforehand, then the party proper, and finally the *nachspill* where you end up in the early hours of the morning. I didn't get invited to them straight away, but once I went to the first one it seemed to lead to a string of them, a whole alternative existence that bloomed between midnight and 6 a.m., hours where you didn't really need to sleep anyway, because it never got dark.

Anyway, it all starts at Huset, and that's where I got to know Petter as well.

Everybody knows (1994)

I am shivering a little as I walk up to Huset. I left my
jacket there earlier in the afternoon. It is only 4°C
out but if you turn up lightly clad they assume you are
already in and don't ask you to pay the cover charge.
And for some reason breaking the rules always seems more
acceptable out on this frontier.

Inside, the curtains are drawn and the lights low.
Candles on the tables. Evening atmosphere. But still
early evening. It's Friday, shrimp night at the restaurant. People cluster around tables laughing, drinking
beer and licking their salty fingers. Later the haunting voice of Kari Bremnes will come on. Leonard Cohen in
Norwegian cover versions mark this summer, but especially Kari Bremnes singing *Everybody Knows*. The opening of
the second verse - *everybody knows the ship is leaking*
- signals the subtle change from evening to night. Time
to move to the miners' bar at the back, where the walls
are black as coal and there are no windows at all. Time
to switch from beer to vodka before the third verse hits:
*everybody knows you've been discreet, but there were so
many people you just had to meet, without your clothes...*

He is there, with his asymmetrical face and hollow cheeks that make him look a bit like a wolf. I know he is with the group of guides working for the German, but not staying in the same shared apartment. They have told me he is living by himself up in Nybyen somewhere.

I have seen him a few times by now. But we spoke for the first time a couple of days ago when I was walking down the valley with the German and he had driven past with a local journalist - it seems there are always people who want to speak to him about something or another. He and the German chatted for a few minutes and then he looked over at me, "Hi, I'm Petter." "Marianne", I replied. He spoke in Norwegian, but his singsong Swedish accent was unmistakeable.

Back to Huset. I think about going over to say hello but there are too many people around him. Mainly women. So I wait until later to orchestrate a trip to the bar at a moment when I see him in conversation with a Norwegian sailor I vaguely know.

"Hey there," I say to the sailor, and then turn to greet his companion, as though it is an afterthought. And somehow we get talking, and are drinking, and the conversation flows, and the sailor goes his way and we don't even really notice he has left. Strains of Leonard Cohen filter through like background light, and by the end of the evening we have the illusion of knowing something about each other.

Petter tells me he is leaving the next day on a 3-week trek up through Dickson Land. He has never been this far north before, although he spent a couple of years in Tromsø working with a local theatre company. He was working as a guide there in his spare time and he

knows about kayaking on white summer nights and camping out in the snow and the lie of the glaciers in the
Lyngsalps area, so there is no reason he should feel
particular apprehension here. Yet he finds the wilderness of Svalbard daunting. Its landscape seems to
defy the superficial imprint of man (and we agree it is
mainly men who have left their traces behind over the
centuries), unlike more southern landscapes that have
been shaped and transformed by millennia of human activity. And then there are the polar bears, and the ice
that can close in around your boat, a glacier that suddenly calves, or just the weather that can change in an
instant and you are far away from anywhere.

Despite the scar tissue left by active coal mines
and the remains of now abandoned operations, prospect-
ing, whaling and more, this is a place that confronts
you as a human and leaves you feeling very small. And I
forget that he seems like a womanizer, or maybe I like
that because it means that I don't have to give anything
too much weight, and his humility in the face of nature
resonates with me. And he listens to me, really listens,
when I tell him how being up here is like living a different reality. A different me. How I open my windows
at night to see the sun spilling into the valley and let
the wind blow into my open mind. And he doesn't ask me
if I am on some sort of acid trip.

And suddenly everything seems possible and he asks
me if I need a lift home and I tell him I came by bicycle so he teasingly asks me for a lift. He jumps onto
the back as I kick off and I can feel his arms around my
ribs as my legs push against the rise in the road towards
Nybyen, but it doesn't make much sense and we tumble off

again and he offers to switch, but then he has his arm around my waist and is pushing the bicycle for me with the other as we walk up instead.

"Will you come in?"

I nod and lean my bicycle by the entrance to his building, I can't remember which block it is now. We don't kiss immediately. We are standing close together, he is looking at me and I am looking away, past him. He asks my permission and I hesitate. We know enough about each other by this time to know we are both transgressing. We each have someone waiting in another place. But that place seems so far away. That time. And I look back at him and catch his gaze. And he smells like nutmeg. And after all, we are ultimately free. I feel I should tell him, "I have my period."

"Is that a problem?" he asks.

"Not if it isn't for you."

And then we stop speaking until much later when we are breathing quietly together, still entwined, on the verge of sleep. "And now what happens?" he smiles, as we slowly draw away from each other. The tangle of sheets and crumpled clothes underneath us fill with blood and I rush to the bathroom. ▰

Jon looks at us, says everything is fuzzy for him, puts an arm around each of our shoulders and gives us a squeeze, "Love you guys." Then he stumbles off to bed.

Renata and I have only had a couple of hours' sleep, but we have a gun lined up for today and are itching to step out beyond the city limits.

After breakfast, we force ourselves to be patient and sit. Where is Tom the Bike? Renata sketches while I write, waiting for Tom to turn up with the gun. He is doing us a favour so we have no leverage to nag. Seems like a no-show, so eventually we resign ourselves to a day of shopping.

"Do you think you perceive time differently in different places?" asks Saskia as we freewheel down to the centre of town. I am used to questions like this from Saskia. She is the sort of person who applies Spinoza to breakfast choices.

"Definitely," I reply. "But do you think there might be more than a subjective difference? I find it weird to think that the earth's spin is about 1600 km/hr at the Equator, but 0 at the poles. I think someone told me it's about 350 km/hr here. Do you think that means we age differently?"

"Only if you think it does," she responds with a smile.

The main store greets us, reassuringly, much the same as it used to be. Svalbardbutikken, the place of many errands and encounters. I remember and imagine chance meetings at the cheese counter, like that time I was not expecting to run into Petter and one of his girlfriends. But this time it is Tom the Bike who taps Renata on the shoulder, "I've got your gun. Do you want me to brief you on how to use it?"

I will also need a briefing, as it has been years since I last held a weapon of any kind.

SIGN ON THE ROAD
LEADING FROM THE
AIRPORT TO TOWN

Gjelder hele
Svalbard

What
does that
sign say ?

ME

It says valid for
the whole of
Svalbard. It's
a bit ironic
but deadly
serious at the
same time.

MARIANNE

MARIANNE TELLS ME SHE HASN'T USED A GUN SINCE SHE WAS
LAST IN SVALBARD 17 YEARS AGO. HOPEFULLY IT'S ONE OF
THOSE SKILLS YOU NEVER FORGET, LIKE RIDING A BICYCLE.

Guns and angels (1994)

"If you are going to spend any time here, you're going to have to learn to shoot." The German has become my guardian angel – I always need a guardian angel – and is also the friend who insists on initiating me into this new skill. It is a scary prospect. I don't like guns. I have never been interested in shooting.

He takes me up to Mine 3, the abandoned mine that has a shooting range behind it where local people practise. There is no one else around. "You are only allowed to shoot in self-defence. And remember, you are not allowed to shoot a bear at a distance of more than 10 metres." If it is further away, you shoot to miss, to scare it away.

Later I will think about this constantly when I am guiding and my more undisciplined tourists start to stray away from the group. But for the moment I focus on learning about the gun. I learn how to load and unload it, how to carry it safely. Next I have to learn to actually shoot. I feel sick in the stomach. I put on the ear muffs, make sure the gun is firmly pressed against my shoulder, take aim as instructed, and fire. The re-

coil takes my breath away. But I realize I like it. It
gives me a visceral buzz to feel the power of the weapon
that I am controlling. My eldest brother likes to tell
people I am a gentle person, but suddenly I understand
a lot of things I had never understood before, not just
about other people, but about myself.

The following year I will come back with Blond
Viking, to practise with other types of guns, including
a .44 Magnum, which I decide is my favourite. Standing
feet apart and holding it with two hands, a fleeting image of Charlie's angels going through my mind before reminding myself that I am being completely ridiculous...
He tells me that this model is the only handgun capable
of killing a bear. You're supposed to have a special
permit to carry it, but he lets me take it sometimes when
I'm going up Nordenskiöldtoppen.

Then there are the old Mausers. Some with small
swastikas carved into the wood. I have a strange feeling
in my gut when carrying these guns from World War II. I
wonder what they have done, what they have witnessed?
Whose hands have held them? Was it better or worse to
die on the battlefield than elsewhere? Somehow I put
the uncomfortable thoughts away and only take them out
occasionally. I also avoid taking these guns out as
much as possible. I am assigned my own rifle, a smaller
and newer Norwegian model, which I carry in a sealskin
pouch made by one of the local trappers. More on seals
later. But don't start me on the arms industry or we'll
be here all day.

Carrying the gun also implies rituals. You load it
only when you leave the town limits. For me that usually means as I go up that road behind Huset towards the

small valley on the side, Tverrdalen. And when you come
back, you unload. The bullets jingle around in jacket
or trouser pockets for the rest of the day. If you go
into a restaurant or a shop, you have to leave your gun
outside. There are racks for that. No one ever seems to
take anyone else's gun, at least not during the years
that I was there. ▚

MARIANNE SPOTTED
AN ARCTIC POPPY

PTARMIGANS

This gun is different to the one I used to use back when I was guiding, but it will do, and finally we can go for a walk. We clamber up the rocky path in Tverrdalen, over the moraine at the bottom of Nordenskiöld glacier and part of the way up the ridge, but decide not to continue upwards. It's only our first day out and the weather is foggy so there's not much of a view today.

Instead we head over the plateau in the direction of the port. Renata enumerates the types of ground underfoot. Stones. Large stones, small stones, gravelly stones, parts that seem like piles of rubble. Polygonal formations of small stones that have been pushed outwards as the top layer of earth thaws in the summer, and tundra-like spongy areas... I had forgotten the relief of the plateau. The discontinuous surface, the discreet snow patches, the small indents and cracks, hints of valleys leading off to one side or the other.

It's late by the time we get home, but Jon has leftovers for us that we devour. He sits drinking tea with us as we eat. "Renata, before you leave, would you draw a portrait of my girlfriend?" he asks. His face lights up as he shows us some photos of her. "Of course," says Renata. "She is a baker," he tells us. "We're planning to have a baby soon." We haven't talked about such personal things before now. I pull out my phone and show Jon photos of my two daughters. I haven't been thinking about them much but suddenly I miss them intensely – will I bring them here one day? Is it possible to connect these worlds?

"How about you? Do you have a family, Renata?" Jon prods.

"I have a teenage son," she replies, "but he is living with his other mother. I only get to see him every second weekend." Renata rarely talks about this with people she doesn't know well. Should I switch the subject? But Jon is listening quietly and respectfully as Renata tells a bit more. "It's been two years now," she comments, "but it still doesn't feel right."

One of Jon's new friends comes over to join us, an intense-looking student with a permanently knitted brow who is writing a thesis on the application of psychoanalytic theory to architecture in the Arctic. Renata stops speaking and our conversation changes tack.

Psy-Girl's theories sound a bit far-fetched, yet as she explains her research her words trigger a series of memories in my mind. I have had strong reactions to specific places which I refrain from sharing for fear of being analysed by this new acquaintance. The lines of violent energy that came out in my sleep when I was staying in Gorée, the island in Senegal that saw the departure of millions of slaves. The bloody nightmares I had when Takao (remember him?) invited a few friends including the Kid and myself to his carpenter's workshop in Normandy – finding out later that a plane had crashed there in World War II. And of course the abstract monsters that people my dreams here in Svalbard.

Jon asks Renata about *feng shui*, and she explains something about the origins of that concept and the accompanying notion of *kan yu*, or the law of heaven and earth. I think about Hiawatha's home on Axeløya, and how it fits in with the lie of the land, the lines of the landscape… and I know that he thought consciously about the alignment when he built it. Every single piece of wood found on the beach and carefully fitted together.

And I start wondering about how personal identity is linked to the land. And my own place in this place that is not mine. Homecoming and yet not home, homecoming yet alienation. Longyear city, translated directly from the Norwegian, is no longer a village, it is actually becoming a city, growing, evolving, and it hasn't even noticed my absence.

I am still tuned in to the conversation around the table yet far enough away that Renata startles me when she asks me to tell the group about my play, and the book we are writing together.

"It's about the human exploitation that transforms places like this. But I haven't gotten very far yet." Although it is not yet a fully human landscape here, the planet is in the throes of changes that stand to fundamentally alter this place.

"But there is hope. Do you know about the seed bank here?" asks Renata. "Or rather seed banks," she adds. Tom the Bike has explained that, in addition to the world-famous Global Seed Vault, the original bank in Mine 3 that I used to take tourists to still exists and is part of a 100-year experiment to test the viability of seeds that are stored there without refrigeration.

Curious how this seemingly barren Arctic land has been designated to safeguard the world's agriculture.

Psy-Girl nevertheless notes the ironic destiny of this place, founded in 1906 as a coal-mining town. Just over a century later the Arctic ice is slowly melting due to the whole planet's unfettered fossil fuel extraction and use. What will this place look like in a century's time?

Jon zooms out even further, "Check out this fossil I found up at the glacier this morning." He pulls from his pocket a sliver of mottled grey stone, engraved with the delicate veins of a leaf. The trace of vegetation from a much warmer period, tens of millions of years ago. The coal seams themselves bear witness to the slow compression of the luxuriant plant life that used to characterize this place. We are so small.

Primeval flora (1994)

My first summer in Longyearbyen is drawing to a close. I have been busy with translations for the store and the museum, accompanying the German and his documentary-maker clients around the place, and learning to know the landscape.

But there is still a week to go and I have some time on my hands, so I muster up my courage to knock on the door of Blond Viking up in Nybyen. I haven't seen him since he pulled up beside me in his car the day after I arrived earlier this month. First door on the left, he had said. I find myself standing on the doorstep, boots muddy, caught in the timelessness that comes with hesitation.

I hear voices, laughter. An Australian accent? That must be the golden boy who dropped his career in high finance for a new life in the Arctic. I have a family connection to Australia and everyone has been telling me I should meet him when he eventually comes back from his field trip. It is a sign. I take a deep breath and knock on the door.

Conversation flows easily. Golden Boy is an easy-going Australian who grew up in the town of Ararat.

I tell him about my teenage years in Orange, another Australian town with a history of agriculture and goldmining. He is friends with Blond Viking and his associate, also a comic-strip Viking, but tall and dark with slightly wild curly hair, a former miner who has turned his local knowledge into a successful guiding business. The Vikings are laughing, mocking Golden Boy about getting too big for his boots and not wanting to work for them anymore. And yes, they do need French-speaking guides. Tall Viking is the senior partner and hires me on the spot for a fossil-plucking walk the next day – I like the way the Norwegian language uses the word "pluck" for the task of picking out the beautiful leaves that were cast in stone way back in the early Tertiary Era, more than 60 million years ago. There is something musical about it. An underlying silent song of time.

This is the easiest of all walks, slow and patient work looking for the leaves and other imprints among the rocks and mud being bulldozed forwards by the glacier as it advances. They hire me for a couple of other small assignments that week. And we agree that I will come back and work for them the following year.

The very last evening I am invited to dinner at Golden Boy's place. There are a bunch of people there, speaking a mixture of English and Norwegian. It feels like home. As I am walking back to my tiny studio I run into Tall Viking, now my new boss. "Is it tedious to say goodbye?" he asks. "Tedious?" *Trasig* – the Norwegian word he uses is new to me, a word that they use up north. "Is it difficult?" Yes, yes it is. Each time I leave a place, a certain universe, it tears me apart inside. ▰

Day 3
Thresholds

"I don't think I'll go out walking today," Renata tells me in the morning. I know better than to insist – sometimes she needs time alone. So I dress and prepare to walk up Nordenskiöldtoppen alone. Nordenskiöld is my favourite summit near Longyearbyen, my special place.

Monday used to be the day for going up there. That was when my weekly 6 p.m. walk was scheduled, perfect to see the late-night sun over the fjord from the summit. Some Mondays I would be feeling lazy and pray that no one would turn up for that walking tour. But someone always did and then I was happy after all.

I pick my way up through the stones in Tverrdalen and take a path that isn't too steep into the moraine at the top. But it seems as though the moraine has crept forward into the valley. Does this make sense? Can there be more moraine and less glacier? Can the heavy machinery of the glacier be grinding down the mountain this fast?

There are Arctic poppy fields up here, the small white blooms shining almost fluorescent against the fine black shards of stone that have almost become earth. Large boulders are scattered throughout the moraine. Some are luminous yellow from within, or bright orange with lichen. They look like tombstones or witnesses to an unknown religion. Maybe some Northern gods have been absent-mindedly playing dice here.

I head up onto the ridge, past where Renata and I had stopped the day before, and beyond, to the spot I remember stopping at the

MARIANNE HAS GONE OUT WALKING BY HERSELF TODAY. I THOUGHT IT MIGHT BE AN OPPORTUNITY TO GET TO KNOW JANIKE, THE RECEPTIONIST, A BIT BETTER, BUT SHE DOESN'T SEEM INTERESTED.

very first time I came up here. I would stop again if I didn't know the place and see the familiar path before me. My fear of heights is talking to me: "Hey, turn around, don't go further." Other voices remind me that this is my familiar mountain. I remember the Young Viking from Toulouse talking me up and I talk myself up now. But it is hard. "Each act is virginal, even repeated," said René Char. Each time is the first time. Seventeen years ago, I was over my fear of heights and walked here confidently. But it was always latent, and without constant effort it is back. This is an easy walk for most people who live around here. Slightly taxing maybe, but not at all scary. For me the physical effort is fine, but my mind is more difficult to master. Nevertheless, as I proceed, the multiple chattering voices gradually quieten down and I get into a sort of flow. I am completely alone. No one else has had the idea to go up here today.

There is no snow patch to cross this time. Just bare earth. I'm not sure if this is seasonal or a sign of change. I can't remember if that top patch used to disappear by August, and it feels wrong that I can't remember.

Wisps of mist greet me at the top, creating a surreal veil over the landscapes in the distance. There is no wind. I sit and drink some sweet tea from the thermos. The silence impresses itself on my ears and eyes. I sit some more, letting go of my thoughts. All the voices have gone quiet now.

Before my body becomes too cold and stiff, I shake my legs and start back down. I can just see a rim of broken stone before me in the mist. I aim for the centre of it, remembering not to stray too close to the glacier on the side that I briefly feared would swallow me the second time I walked up here.

A small crevasse (1995)

And so at the beginning of the summer of 1995, I come back. My memories are unreliable and I cannot recall my arrival. Is it Tall Viking who picks me up?

This year I am living in a compact bedsit in Nybyen, at the top of the valley, maybe it is in Block 2 (the buildings in Nybyen that used to house the miners are set up as blocks filled with tiny units). Some of my time is spent translating, some writing. Some guiding.

My very first guiding assignment is up to the top of Nordenskiöldtoppen. It will be one of my regular routes. My walk up there the year before is engraved in my memory. But it is not the crinoline of rock and snow that I scaled last time I was in Longyearbyen. This early in the season the bony ridge is fully wrapped in thick drapes of white.

So Tall Viking decides that someone should show me the best route to take at this time of year, and calls on the Student, a young man who has been to the top many times and who brings a couple of friends along too.

"Just follow me." So we do. About 10 minutes into the trip he admits he has never actually walked up here before. He will just lead us up the route that he usually takes with his snowmobile, diagonally across the glacier and up the ridge on the opposite side. I am a little uneasy about walking straight over the snow-blanketed glacier in this way, but he assures me it's fine.

It is quite easy to get to the top and the snow along the ridge somehow makes it seem safer, softer, less icy. We fan out a little as we come down towards the ridge on the Longyearbyen side, and suddenly my left leg slides down into a slippery place. No foothold. My leg is obviously no longer on solid mountain but in a crevasse. I still have a hold with my right leg, but I can't get out and am afraid of slipping. This could be a small crack or it could be a gaping crevasse that goes all the way down to the heart of the glacier. I call out to the Student, who comes over and hauls me out. We don't talk much about it but I wonder how close I was to some horrible incident.

When I tell the story to Tall Viking later he nearly jumps out of his skin. "You're lucky you didn't all disappear into the glacier!"

From then on I take that walk myself, and I follow the route I know from my first trip up. It always goes well, except maybe for the time when I am with a Swiss tourist and we get down off the moraine to find ourselves in thick fog. I do not know where I am. The terrain is such that it isn't really possible to get totally lost ("Seriously - lost on the moraine?" says Tall Viking later. I wonder if I am going to lose my job for being so hopeless, the Bridget Jones of guiding in the Arctic...). You will come to a place that goes either up or down soon enough. But I don't want to accidentally take us down a precipice. So

I suggest we sit down and have a cup of tea and a biscuit until the fog lifts. Which is what we do. And the fog lifts enough at one point for me to realize exactly where we are. "You were so calm," the Swiss tourist says later.

There are other walks. Like the ominous-sounding but relatively easy ones up to the Troll Stone or to the Sarcophagus. Once Petter and I go to the Troll Stone together to take photographs of the curious rock formation that sits perched at the top of the ridge. On the way down the sun gives us a rainbow halo, concentric rings of colour creating a perfect circle around our shadows projected onto the mist below. "We must be saints," he teases, knowing well that we are not.

On another walk, up to the Sarcophagus this time, I am guiding a French family – as the only French speaker I tend to get the French tourists. It is the 14th of July, French national day. The family appears to be recently blended and the man and woman have eyes only for each other. Both sporting the most up-to-date mountain gear, whereas the two 10-year-old girls in tow are in lightweight tennis shoes that soon become soaked through.

The man leaves a bottle of champagne in a rivulet on the glacier so it will have time to chill by the time we return. Perfect for a unique celebration. He and she then waltz off, despite my countless reminders to stay with the group. I make sure the children are okay at least, lifting them over the meltwater channels, doing my best to keep their feet out of water. A little further up I run into Petter with his own group – he grins at me shouting as the couple disappears up the slope.

When I get back to that spot on our way down, the champagne is gone. Did Petter remove the bottle, or was it just washed down by the current? I imagine it being spat back out by the glacier centuries - or, who knows, millennia - down the track, like Ötzi the Iceman.

The Frenchman is furious. He curses and swears, and finally proceeds in silence. Everyone stays close to me from then on.

I also have soaked feet by the time we get back. I peel off my socks and sit on the steps of the office at Block 1. Petter has turned up and is in the office, chatting with Tall Viking and Blond Viking. He opens the door but doesn't say a word about the champagne and I choose not to ask. Instead he steps outside with a bottle of Gilde aquavit, breaks the seal and hands me a shot glass. We sit together for a moment in the cool air, my belly warm and my bare feet steaming slightly, and any remaining frustration with the tourists melts away. Gilde tastes of that evening. Or the other way around.

Was that the year that Viking Girl was there too? Or was that the following year? Strapping and energetic, with rosy red cheeks, from the south of Norway, up in Svalbard for the first time. She was so cheerful and kind. "The sort of girl you should get married to," says Blond Viking, meaning himself, but then has second thoughts, "No, she is so thirsty for adventure, it wouldn't be good for her." Surely she's the one who gets to decide, I think. I wonder what she is doing now?

I had promised to get my driver's licence but I still don't have it. So Viking Girl does all the driving. Taking people out to walk through the valley at the end of the road, Bjørndalen, or over to see Mine 7 and the satellite dish. And I do some of the office work when I am not out on walks.

And then there are the two young French women that
Blond Viking takes on tour, who have gotten themselves
a magazine assignment sponsored by a cosmetic company.
Hair and make-up always perfect for photo shoots in the
Zodiac, suitably framed by glaciers and icebergs. They
seem unattainably worldly and enterprising. "Not as
tough as you," says Blond Viking.

In the beginning I was a bit dismissive of Blond
Viking. He seemed like a surf head, the more frivolous of
the two partners. But after working with him for a while
the initial clichéd comic-strip image starts to fade. I
like helping him with tasks like building the wooden roof
of a new warehouse. I am not very skilled but he gives me
the simple task of pencilling in the lines where he needs
to cut the wood, and he is patient. Our conversation blooms
and then dies down again in natural cycles, without being
forced, sort of like when you rope up to cross a glacier.

Another day, maybe a year later, when he and Tall
Viking have gone their separate ways – we sit together
in an attic above a stable and sort through mouldy bread
for the horses that he has just bought as part of his
newest venture. We have been sharing an apartment for a
while and have a sort of easy intimacy. He is comfortable if I need to come in and pee while he is in the shower – and vice versa. In the mornings he remembers his
dreams and we talk about them – or I tell him mine. He
confides in me sometimes about relationships and other
life questions, but that day we talk about Petter. "Ah,
so he's the one. That's why he keeps turning up at the
office," he muses. "Yes, he's the man."

But I am not so sure that Petter is the man, at least
for me – and I can't understand what he is really looking

for, if anything. He is even more restless than I am. I can't really say that there is anything between us, yet he seeks me out every time he is back in town. And he challenges me, which I like.

"I'm sure he cares about you – you are so *vrien og vrang*," says Blond Viking. So twisted and mixed up. Or stubborn and clever? Or something else again?

"What do you mean?" I ask.

"I mean it would be hard to get bored with you," he replies. I still don't really understand but it sounds like a compliment. ▨

THE HOSTEL COMMON ROOM IS WHERE WE EAT
AND TALK ABOUT STUFF.

My thigh muscles are complaining but I descend quite quickly.

How did I manage to forget that I don't go walking in the mountains any more? It is only when Renata asks me about this that I realize the last time was probably the last time I was in Svalbard. Maybe even this peak. Yet my body responds. It seems to know the steps, the movements. And somehow the streets and the steps of the city I live in seem to have kept me fit enough.

I am ravenous when I get back from my walk, but we find ourselves without food. Renata had left our provisions in the "leftovers" area of the communal fridge, and we discover a young French couple cooking up all the ingredients we needed for our *arroz chaufa*, the Peruvian equivalent of Cantonese fried rice and Renata's signature dish. We have been craving it ever since the evening we spent discussing Cantonese food with Kevin, who has just texted us to let us know that he will be with us soon – it's his last evening in Longyearbyen. But all we have left now is the rice.

"Didn't you see the sign in the fridge?" I grumble.

"You're the local, you should tell me how things work around here. Anyway, you know my English isn't great." Renata refuses to be held responsible. As for the couple, they don't look keen to give up their winnings. Somehow it is sorted out – they hadn't eaten it all, and Jon has some leftovers he's happy to share – so we re-seal the frayed ends of our tempers. Kevin is a bit disappointed he won't get to taste this famous Peruvian variation on Chinese cuisine, but we agree that we will meet up again somewhere, some day, to make it up to him. I'm sorry Kevin – I'm not sure we'll keep that promise.

Around us the common room is humming with different languages, a mix of ethnicities, a crossing of different personal paths, including the Thais who have made this Arctic town their home. "Perfect for you, the former anthropology student!" Renata teases. But here, as elsewhere, it is difficult to be both within and without, a participant and an observer. And who do I identify with anyway? The Norwegians from Oslo,

where I was born, the French travellers from the city where I live, the Australians from the city I grew up in, or the people who live here? Although I am theoretically in my home country, the Thai woman who keeps tabs on the dining room is more of a local than I am.

An older Asian-looking man approaches Renata and says something to her in Japanese. She apologizes and confesses that she only knows a few words. He looks disappointed and moves away. "At least this time I didn't have to tell my whole life story," she comments. She is regularly approached by Japanese people, used to being mistaken for something that she is not, yet it is always a bit painful.

"I feel I should be able to relate more," she often tells me. "After all, my parents are first-generation immigrants." I recognize her discomfort; this understanding is part of our friendship – the feeling of being caught between identities and the expectations of others.

"I don't even speak Spanish like a native anymore," she remarks to the group. "I realized when I was in China that learning Cantonese made me more aware of the logic of language in general, including the flaws in my written and spoken Spanish. Years later when I returned to Peru, one of my cousins said to me: 'Renata, you no longer have a Peruvian accent... and it seems like you think before you speak.' Of course he meant that I chose my words carefully and didn't sound as spontaneous as before. And he was right. But I couldn't resist answering, 'Yes Rony, some people *do* think before they speak.'"

We all laugh, but there is a serious note in her words. And I take heart in the thought that being able to distance oneself can also be a strength – alienation lends perspective, like in the theatre of Brecht.

I am back to wondering about my own place in this land of mine that is not. Returning and yet not home. This town that took me in all those years ago, where I found work and adventure and friendship with a synchronicity worthy of magic realism.

The Tall Viking I used to work for now lives in France. One day out of the blue, a phone call – I still don't know how he found me – after a silence of more than 10 years, "I've just moved to Paris! I'm married now, and my wife left her job in Svalbard for a new assignment in Paris so I followed her." So much news in one go. So incongruous that he should be living in my city, so strange and upside-down. Yet somehow he reopened that door to the north for me, without which I would not be here now.

Paris and Longyearbyen reconnected via a special wormhole. Maybe the same wormhole that made Magdalena fjord famous in an advertising campaign that splashed giant photographs of the site all over the Paris metro. A campaign probably organized by the company his wife is now working for.

The northernmost settlement (1993)

We arrive in Ny Ålesund the next day, just off 79°
north. A completely different geology here, where the
forces at work have shaped pointed peaks that rise up
before us. As for the settlement, the tiny cluster of
buildings appears as a strange and fragile outpost of
human enterprise.

Everyone spills off the cruise ship at the same time.
It seems like an insult to both the land and the community,
suddenly overrun by voices and questions and footprints.

The community seems to think the same thing. I assume I will have a privileged status as the only one
from the ship who speaks Norwegian (the ice pilot has
stayed on board), but the scientists and others who live
and work here are just as stand-offish with me as with
everyone else.

One of them is nevertheless kind enough to lend me a
bicycle (probably to get rid of me) and I go off exploring as far as the short road will lead me, all the time
keeping an eye out for bears. The tourists are mainly
milling around the quay area and seem impressed that I
have found a means of locomotion.

The Kid from Paris, my lonesome policeman friend – the one who triggered the whole series of events that led me to being here – has asked me to take photos of myself with an Arctic beer can wherever I travel. This is the beer that he imports into France, featuring a polar bear and the mention that it is brewed in the northernmost brewery in the world. I have a can with me now. As this is as far north as I have ever been and – as far as I know then – will probably ever get, I prop up my old Voigtländer camera – the one that had belonged to my father and still has his initials engraved on the top – on a rock, frame the shot, set off the timer and run back to the chosen spot brandishing my beer in the air. A nearby family of barnacle geese eye me suspiciously but decide I am not a threat – my photo captures their beautifully ruffled derrieres in the background. I am even graced with the brief sight of an Arctic fox that trots casually by a little later.

I don't ever go to Ny Ålesund again, although I do end up travelling further north in the following years.

We board the ship and manoeuvre back out, stopping only to admire Magdalena fjord and the mountains arranged behind in superimposed triangles. A calm place. There are lazy seals basking on floating beds of ice that have calved from the glacier. They slip into the water now and again and tessellations of triangles ripple in the mirror.

The boat turns, and we head back towards the continent, and the night. ▨

Jon grabs a few more beers from his stock in the fridge. It's the same Arctic beer I remember, although these are in bottles. He is curious to learn more about the Paris-Longyearbyen wormhole and I tell him about the Kid and the Arctic beer, and Blond Viking and Tall Viking, and how Tall Viking put me in touch with Tom the Bike, and how that's how Renata and I ended up where we are right now, talking to him.

In the meantime, Kevin and Renata are having a separate conversation in Cantonese and the Japanese man from before is looking over at our table, confused.

Jon is wound up from a previous conversation and wants me to take a stance, "So what do you really think about all the recent development here?" he asks. Renata and Kevin stop speaking and also look at me.

I feel caught out. I like to take things lightly, and I've never been an activist, despite secretly aspiring to be. I've said this before. Things have changed here and it scares me. But not only am I a lightweight, I am also an outsider – and expressing any kind of opinion, telling any story, bears a weight of responsibility, a duty of respect that I am not sure I can fully accomplish.

And yet I feel a compulsion to say something. So I spit it out into my writing. Or at least I try.

"What are the options for this place? If development is inevitable, then what kind of development is right?" Renata asks. I don't know.

When I arrived in the nineties, the town was in transition, with mining gradually making way for tourism. My fluency in a few languages and sense of adventure stood in for real qualifications and I was able to pick up the rest on the job, like many others did at the time. There was a frontier town atmosphere and there still is something of that animating the place. A place where individual desires and quests for self-realization cross paths with geopolitical interests and other prevailing currents.

Tonight I am too tired to wrap my mind around these questions. And too tired to write. Or that's what I tell myself. I just want to take refuge in sleep. The others decide to go over to Huset for a last drink before Kevin leaves, and I am happy to have the dorm to myself. As I drift off, it occurs to me that I am still using the same sleeping bag I bought in Longyearbyen way back when. The one that crossed the Barents sea with me twice.

The second crossing (1995)

Tall Viking and Blond Viking are both out with a film crew, Viking Girl is driving some tourists around, and I am alone in the office. I am sitting in Tall Viking's chair, working on some translations for next season's brochure. The mountain is behind me, invisible from where I am. My field of vision spans the angle from the computer on the desk to the window that looks down over the valley.

A woman comes in from the dirt road that leads up from the valley. Red jacket framed in the doorway as she stamps her feet, leaving small cakes of mud on the mat. "Can you 'elp me?"

I respond in French, taking my cue from her accent. We chat. I am drinking a glass of blackcurrant cordial, the typical Norwegian *saft*, and at one point I offer her a drink too. Or at least she tells me that I did - I still harbour feelings of guilt from this encounter. That I was not hospitable enough. That she was too generous with me.

She is trying to contact the skipper of a French yacht that sails in these waters. I know him and had just been thinking about him, wondering whether I could hitch a ride back to the continent in exchange for work as a deckhand, and I remark on this coincidence to her. "Well, I'll mention it to him," she says, "but he already has crew. I have come up here to work on the boat." Her words establish a definite distance, but I can see a smile in the crinkles around her ocean eyes. Saskia is a mariner from way back. And a destiny interchange kind of person.

Somehow it all comes together and a couple of weeks later I am on the yacht, setting sail – or rather motor for the moment. Saskia, the Skipper and me, plus three paying tourists from France. I have learned a few knots and assured the Skipper that I don't suffer from seasickness. He smiles with his slightly crooked teeth. In his book attitude is the most important factor, a certain level of grit, and he assumes I have that.

We don't hit the open ocean immediately. We follow the coast down, accompanied by a consort of fulmars and kittiwakes, stopping first at Barentsburg.

Barentsburg is one of the two remaining Russian settlements in activity at that time. That day it is a vision of greyness, rain and mud. We hitch a ride from the seafront with a truck freighting coal back towards town. The driver's face and lips are the same colour as the sky. He wears a moth-eaten woollen coat that used to be black over a couple of layers of sweatshirts.

His eyes are focused on the potholes and muddy edges to make sure that the truck reaches its destination. I make an attempt to speak with him in my rudimentary Russian but our conversation quickly peters out. The tourist who is with me makes a disparaging remark and

I hope that the driver doesn't have unsuspected French language skills.

We arrive at a grey concrete building with a cluster of men at the door. I recognize one of them, the Georgian I had met during my first season in Longyearbyen at the official interpreter's residence. Another younger man's face stands out in the crowd. A dreamer's face. It looks paler, softer than the others', his eyes a hint of blue pastel in the otherwise colourless landscape.

A subtle smell of coal hangs in the 45 percent humidity. Next to the statue of Lenin there is an array of blocks that used to display the photos of the best workers. Now they are gathering coal dust.

We are shown around. The gymnasium is a cold room with high ceilings, some ropes and a couple of exercise machines from another decade. The canteen smells of pork. We visit the pigsty too, which smells even stronger. These pigs are indoors for the term of their abridged lives, destined to end up on the plates of the Russian and Ukrainian miners who live in this northern town, although probably not worse off than the bulk of factory pigs anywhere else.

The Dreamer tells us of his life here. He is studying English and Norwegian, saving his better-than-average earnings for a better life. Later he will come and visit us in France.

There are patches of blue between the clouds as we return to the port. The sea is as smooth as glass, projecting the image of the naked mountains into its depths. We switch on the motor and glide away.

Our next halt is at Bellsund, our first meeting with Hiawatha. But I have already told you about that.

Further south. A glacier shining in the blue light. The signature fat seals lying around on blocks of ice at the face of the glacier with its twisted towers, bobbing up and down a little when a chunk breaks off. We sail up to a sort of indent in the ice where we see water splashing around dark openings in the ice. The gateway to something we decide to call the Inner Arctic. The darkness invites us to enter, but we might not ever come back out.

Our last venture ashore before the crossing. Only Saskia and I disembark. It is a rock more than anything. A reef near the south of the island. Has anyone else ever set foot here I wonder now? We pull the Zodiac up onto a small beach. There is a photo of this moment. I am standing on the reef in a shaft of light with the open sea behind me, rifle on my shoulder. Is this a dream? A feeling that will come back to me many years later as I watch the sun rise on Mount Kinabalu, on the island of Borneo.

The wind is up and we are in full sail as we make our way southwards. I know nothing about managing the sails but I learn how to follow instructions and have stamina at the wheel. On my first watch I am the only person awake on the boat. After months of daylight, we have just hit the edge of night as we gear down into less boreal latitudes.

And then the dolphins. Strange silver beasts leaping before the bow, a V-shape across their backs. I wake the others, who climb out of bed, "Are you sure you're not hallucinating? It's a well-known phenomenon for novice sailors..." and we admire the shiny creatures leaping before us into the dusk.

The hours blur as we alternate watches of four hours. Night sailing. The boat is on a swift steady course.

At one point I am woken during the night to help with a manoeuvre, taking a reef. I'm not quite sure what this means but follow instructions. My task is simple but key. If I let the sheet slip my skipper will fall from the mast and everything will go wrong. At sea, trust is fundamental.

I am a bit slow and the Skipper almost berates me. This is no time for the sailor's conditional, the slow "could have been" tense I learned the day before which refers to an opportunity already passed, like "we could have given her a bit more sail there".

Then it is time to change watch. I slip into my warm sleeping bag as someone else climbs out. My sleeping sheet is an eiderdown cover I've had since I was a child. Midnight blue with clusters of stars. It becomes a magic carpet that launches each of us into flight as we slide into sleep. We share brief snippets of our dream worlds as we swap places again to take advantage of each other's residual warmth.

We play with words and write the water into our diaries. This crossing is a life poem.

It takes three days, but I cannot remember daylight. Or eating. Just sailing and sleeping and slipping into the bed of stars.

On the evening of the third day, we sight land. We all get up, go out on deck, and the Skipper puts on the Rolling Stones, really loud. We latch on to the ladder leading up to the cockpit, swaying to *Paint It, Black*, slightly drunk on darkness and sleeplessness.

And suddenly the sea is calm again, with a belt of islands protecting us from the ocean. I am at the wheel and Saskia and the Skipper guide me through the maze of lighthouses.

Later as we start to follow the coast we will meet people. One fisherman's net becomes tangled in our propeller. I cannot remember the details, but we close the story by atoning with two bottles of good wine from our cellar. Saskia and I row over to him, across the choppy sea. He looks bewildered when our two faces peer up from below, offering Australian and French wines, but accepts our gifts with willing wonderment. We imagine him re-telling an embellished version of the story in the pub that night, "these two sirens appeared from the sea..."

In the Lofoten islands we come across an Italian silversmith in a remote workshop: they call him "Michele the myth", or so he tells us. He worked as a fisherman when he first arrived in Norway many years ago. But Norwegians are taciturn compared to Italians and fishers even more so. It took him five years to learn the language because his companions hardly spoke. We tell him we have sailed down from Svalbard. "Do you know the diamond cutter there?" he asks. There is only one. And yes, we've met. "Say hello then, next time you're up there. He's a friend of mine." We assure him we will, although I'm not sure we ever did.

Yesterday we anchored near a small island. Calm, calm water, cobalt blue evening. As the others prepare the fire I walk through the forest picking blueberries and *molter*. These are golden berries, rare, nestling under protective leaves at ground level, never more than one on each plant. Some say they were even used as currency in the Middle Ages.

There are mushrooms too. My tongue is still burning from the poisonous one I accidentally bit into. But this doesn't prevent me from savouring the fish freshly grilled on the fire.

That was supposed to be followed by tea that Saskia was brewing, but she manages to tip the last pot onto the fire, almost extinguishing it and earning her the nickname "wet blanket".

And now we are sailing again, sporadically surrounded by puffins - simultaneously elegant and comical with their large red beaks - as we pass Harstad. Every Norwegian I met in Longyearbyen seemed to be from Harstad, the town is a sort of springboard to the high north. I sit at the round table to write my diary and in the square of blue above me I can see the Skipper at the wheel in his wraparound sunglasses.

Nights, our path across the water is as clear as day, lit by a full moon dangling like a globe in the newly deep darkness. And for the first time I see a shimmering whiteness with a tinge of green flowing through the sky, the aurora, lifting us up into dream reality like a spaceship.

Bodø. This is where I leave the boat to return to land, ultimately the city. I came at the solstice and it is now the equinox. A quarter of a year without traffic lights.

I loosen the ropes, throwing them to my travelling companions as the boat leaves in a cloud of gulls. As I walk along the train tracks to the station, I feel a nausea welling up in me, landsickness. ▨

Day 4
Ghosts

Tuesday is a sunny lazy Longyearbyen day. Pleasurably sore muscles, slow morning, long breakfast. I scroll through the news on my phone. As Renata doesn't have a phone, I update her on the main headlines. "People are really addicted to their phones," she comments. Yes, I am.

"But don't you think that your sketchbook fulfils the same function?" I counter. "It keeps you busy when you have nothing else to do. It is your way of processing reality. And a way of connecting with other people. Just like a phone, right?" She half agrees. It had already occurred to her.

But I know she is thinking that I am wasting time. Why am I not writing more? This trip was supposed to be about writing, not a summer holiday.

Kevin flew out early this morning and has been replaced in our room by a lanky young Norwegian travel enthusiast, 100 countries and counting. I wonder whether he will count Svalbard as a separate country.

Jon, who has been moved to a different floor, turns up and joins us at our table. He has booked a boat tour to the Russian settlement of Barentsburg, and Renata and I decide to bike down to Golden Boy's place. I haven't seen or exchanged a word with Golden Boy in 17 years, but I feel he is somehow part of my story, even if I don't really feature in his. Hiawatha has told me he is in town and explained where the office is, on the corner marked by the polar bear sculpted in strips of bright silver metal.

The door is open and we start taking off our shoes in the entrée, which seems to be the right thing to do. A man appears, "Can I help you?" He has something of a city-dweller's aura and at first I don't recognize him. He doesn't recognize me at all. But then it clicks for me, I explain who I am and he also remembers – it's the kind of town where casual acquaintances from the past do pop up now and again. I introduce Renata too, we stand chatting for a minute, and Renata and I accept his offer of coffee. It is the completely natural magic of Longyearbyen that Hiawatha happens to pop in at that moment (or is it that he saw our bicycles propped up against the wall outside?) and we sit around on the deep sofas holding mugs of coffee, legs tucked up, catching up on each other's lives (he commutes from London) and talking about the way that things have changed.

It occurs to me that it is probably the presence of us outsiders that brings up this talk of change, but also that what they see is probably very different to what I see. I am like the distant aunt on a visit, exclaiming about the nephew who has shot up, but they are the real family of this place, acquainted with the details of the fevers and the sore toes.

They are talking the talk of old timers. These days, there are more stupid people doing stupid things, they say, more unnecessary rescue operations, including for locals. And of course with that comes a greater expectation of rescue and the governor's office monitors everything closely. It used to be different. Hiawatha reminisces about the time he had missed the last provision boat back to town one September and decided to stay where he was until the first ice came. No one even thought about looking for him until some time in November.

I think back to my summer on the rented yacht, but I don't mention it, maybe for fear of being relegated to the category of stupid people doing stupid things.

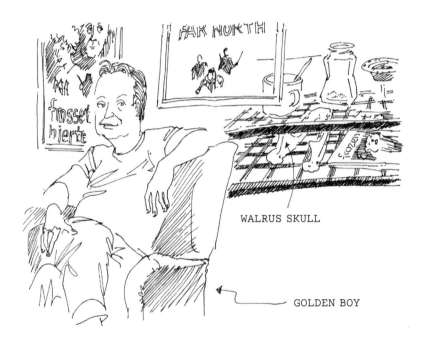

WALRUS SKULL

GOLDEN BOY

The third crossing (1997)

The Skipper had suggested that I come back the following year to work with them. He had a lot of bookings, so he would have two boats. Skipper Jr would captain a rented one and I would assist. I assumed I would get on with Skipper Jr just as well as I did with his older brother. I didn't know much about him, but he had excellent sailing credentials, which was more than I had. So I said yes, of course.

We are picking up the rental in Ålesund, and from there we will sail up over the Barents Sea to Svalbard. A few days at sea. I am not overly concerned. After all, I have done this before.

We agree to meet somewhere in Oslo, but I can no longer remember exactly where. Skipper Jr looks a bit like his brother, slim build, not very tall, and he has the same lilting Breton accent. He is a bit more shy than Skipper Sr but nevertheless makes it clear that he is keen to hit the road straight away. He drives and I help navigate, I think we are in that van that Skipper Sr used to use. It takes us a while to get through the tangle of ring roads around the city and then we are finally on the highway, first north towards Hamar and Lillehammer and then gradually curving westwards.

That night we find a spot somewhere in the middle of nowhere to park the van and sleep in the back, each squeezed into a sleeping bag on either side of the boxes of provisions, barely exchanging a word, and the next day we drive on. Looking back, I have little recollection of the countryside. We go through some beautiful scenery, but it isn't the kind of trip where I feel I can ask to stop to take photos. Skipper Jr is focused on getting to our destination, and seems to think of Norway as a somewhat hostile terrain to get through as fast as possible, a place of incomprehensible language and people. I would like to be a passeur, but I can't find the right words.

And then finally we descend into picturesque and colourful Ålesund where we are to pick up the yacht. A postcard town, with strings of islands covered with coloured houses like children's building blocks bobbing in the bath.

We meet the Sailor by the shed. He is the cliché of the grizzled seaman, a lowslung wifebeater singlet revealing his muscular shoulders and sailor's beer belly. He takes us on board Anna Karenina and explains in thick dialect a lot of arcanely labelled buttons - Skipper Jr and I hope we grasped the essentials.

What the Sailor doesn't tell us is that the floor of the cockpit, the part of the deck where you stand and steer the boat, immediately above the inside dining area, is not actually attached to the boat. Which means the boat will certainly sink if we happen to capsize. But we discover that later, well into our crossing.

Skipper Jr frowns and mutters as he takes over the vessel. She isn't anything like the sleek racing yachts he's used to. I think she's ok but I really don't have many references. I elect to sleep in the dining area, there is an inviting little nook behind a curtain. "Ah, my favourite spot too," says the Sailor. "That's where I always sleep." I guess we have something in common. Skipper Jr chooses one of the cabins in the bow.

Our crewmates join us aboard a day or two later, just as we finish stocking up the boat. Two unknown quantities found via a network of keen amateur sailors who sign up to help deliver boats from one port to another. One is a freshwater sailor, raised on the Swiss lakes. The others tease him a bit, "You're not a real sailor!", but he has years of experience and a storm on the lakes can be formidable. The other is a phlegmatic IT guy from Brittany who likes to sail in his spare time.

I don't recall sailing close to land as we follow the Norwegian coast northwards. But I do remember a last stop, a small island called Finnøya, before striking out on the open sea. I decide to walk up the hill in the centre of the island - I need some time by myself before locking in for this trip with three men I barely know. We are close to the Arctic circle, but it's a balmy evening with a gentle breeze blowing. I criss-cross the slope until I reach the top. Next to the pile of stones that characterizes every Norwegian hilltop, there is a funny little letterbox. I would have left a note, but for once I don't have either pen or paper in my shirt pocket.

Are you still with me, Auden? You said that each port had a name for the sea, or was it poet?

I say that each harbour
is a homecoming
each departure a tearing apart

I climb tonight for the last time
the hilltop of my childhood
the heather springs back from my tread
as I pass
the plants rustle
do I cause them pain?

my breasts ache
my nipples burn like hot stones

the roots that protrude
from the folds of the rocks
are white like bones
each sapling is a lamp

the evening is soft as glass
the evening is luminous
I have left the full moon in the south

I think back to my life in Paris, another universe, and
to my last week there. Looking back, I would be hard
pressed to connect these separate spheres of my life or
remember that they correspond to the same time period,
but the small bare tree trunks that mark the landscape
at this latitude remind me of the branches that I went
looking for with the Kid and an artist friend of his in
the Bois de Vincennes just a couple of Sundays ago. As
a side gig to importing beer, he is redecorating one

of the bars he works with and his friend will be making light fixtures from the fallen branches.

I'm not really nervous, but I know it will be a while before I am immersed in this woody earthy mainland smell again.

It is time to leave. Skipper Jr has studied the weather patterns and reckons that we can circle around the winds and cruise into Longyearbyen from the west so we set out accordingly. The first 24 hours are relatively uneventful. The sea is choppy. Skipper Jr is going over his navigation plan and the other two are vomiting. I don't feel so good myself, but the connectedness of being part of the steering mechanism makes me feel better so I'm happy to be at the wheel so long as I am not expected to make any big decisions.

When is it that the wind starts to turn and stiffen? It slowly grows like an unexpected monster hatched between ocean and sky.

At least we don't have to worry about darkness. It's close to the solstice, and beyond the Arctic Circle the sun no longer even dips below the horizon. But soon we are all suffering from fatigue and lack of sleep. We are doing 2-hour watches and I can barely get my feet warm in the depths of my Arctic-grade sleeping bag when it is already time to climb out again and slip on my clammy rubber boots. We can't heat the boat when it is at this angle, so it is 7°C inside and our damp clothes never quite dry out. And there is not the camaraderie of warming each other's sleeping bags that I experienced on my previous crossing.

It is my watch. I stand in the cockpit - by this time we know it's not attached - watching 5-metre waves take shape above me before they crash onto the deck. Skipper Jr is coaching me, "Take them at 45°, if you're head on you'll explode the sail, but too far sideways and the boat will roll."

I am concentrating so hard that I don't even turn my head when the waves break over me, until he reminds me that I am allowed to look away for a moment to avoid having the water smash into my face. And have less of it trickle down the neck of my oilskin. That's a bit better.

I'm not sure how long this goes on. It seems like forever, and yet time doesn't weigh on me. I am reduced to a sailing machine. Imperfect, but perfectly focused. The only thing that matters is standing here with my feet braced as I turn the wheel to meet each incoming wave. This is a moment I will often look back on later in life, other concerns small or trivial in comparison.

But the atmosphere on the boat is slowly taking on a new character. Freshwater from Switzerland takes me aside. "How long have you known this skipper?" he asks. "Do you really trust him?"

I respond calmly. We are in this together. But he insists, "I have a flight to catch in three days. I don't think we will arrive in time. We should call for rescue."

Around this time we come close to a Russian vessel. It passes us like a ghost ship. Eerie sunlight shines obliquely through the portholes under the dark leaden cloud cover as it rides up and down the waves like a shadow puppet or crude anime. There is no sign of life. No radio contact.

But we have no need of contact really, or rescue. We are holding to our course, and the wind and waves are starting to calm down now. When not at the wheel,

Skipper Jr spends his time bolting things together and making minor repairs. I hear him kick the deck at one point, "Anna Karenina, I hate you." Somehow this worries me more than anything else up until now.

Sunlight, more and more sunlight now. And lead-coloured seas. The slanted rays that are filtering through the clouds are caressing the waves into a kind of calm. Until we are - effectively - becalmed. We've been blown too far east and can't sail upwind to the south cape. And we don't have enough fuel on board to use the motor to get us all the way there. There is nothing for it but to wait. A large glaucous gull glides by effortlessly - is it mocking us?

I am mostly cooking when not asleep or at the wheel. At one point while preparing tea, I hear Freshwater talking to the Breton, "We should take over the boat. Call for rescue. What are they doing?" He is referring to Skipper Jr and me. "I need to get back home. I'm going to miss my flight."

"If we miss our flights, we'll get another flight," responds the Breton phlegmatically. And there is really no danger now. It is just a question of time.

Finally the wind picks up enough again to tack our way towards the north. My gestures are on autopilot and I lapse into contemplation as I stand at the helm.

The degrees are rising, I count each minute
I long to touch the gelid flanks
of the colourless peaks
comb the strands of the cold foreshores
speak the tongue of the land

let the sheets slide
release the flickering light birds
free to spell the lie of the wind
as I lay the lines
to the invisible stars
sway to the slow swell
of the heavy seas

the degrees are rising, I count each minute
chill coast with glittering glaciers of grit and ice
still, you resist with grace

Eventually we sail through the entrance to Isfjord
and arrive at the port of Longyearbyen. Skipper Sr is
there, waiting for us at the quay. We haven't been able
to communicate but he has been scanning the horizon every day for our arrival. There is so much to tell him.
Not all at once. And not with everyone together. He can
read from our weary faces that we did not have the best
of crossings.

The yacht situation gets worse that summer. The
depth-sounder soon breaks down, followed by the radar,
in addition to a cockpit that is barely clinging to the
rest of the vessel.

So Skipper Sr and I go to the governor's office to
understand our rights vis-à-vis the company that rented
us the vessel.

Walking through the administrative building, we
barely take in the various artworks and pictures that
grace the long corridor, until a framed display of knots
catches our eye. I stare, an image of Anna Karenina is
the background of the display, and the artwork is signed

by the Sailor. How did these knots infiltrate the governor's office? What does it all mean?

I'll probably never know what weird space-time tangle caught up with me there. ▨

Golden Boy wanders out to answer a phone call and Hiawatha has a lightbulb moment as he watches Renata finishing off a drawing in her sketchbook. Could she design a logo for him? For his *Top Down* eiderdown business? That tuft of down he showed me the other day, collected from nests at his old trapper station in Akseløya – he has much more hidden away, enough for about 100 eiderdowns. Yes, ok, we'll drop by later today or tomorrow. I am enthusiastic, delighted that we will be giving something back to Longyearbyen. Well, actually, it is Renata who will be giving back on behalf of both of us. Not quite sure what she thinks really.

"What *do* you think about it, Renata?" I ask belatedly.

"It's ok. I'll do it."

After we leave, we decide to stop by Svalbardbutikken. We make it beyond the food section this time, ending up in the part with all the books. *Svalbard Birds* stands out and I pick it up. Petter and I had been leafing through it that night on the boat when we spoke about Aristophanes and the birds.

Echos (1996)

It is my second last summer in Longyearbyen. Hiawatha the trapper has become a friend now. I think. It is always a little hard to tell if you meet his stringent friendship criteria. Every now and again I catch him judging me and finding me wanting. But then forgiving me for my inadequacies. I am just a city girl after all.

He has asked Skipper Sr for help bringing some gear down to his cabin and I am tagging along. Even though I am mainly working for Tall Viking and Blond Viking now, I manage to squeeze in a few sailing assignments in between. Petter is going too. He will be staying with Hiawatha to help collect the down left by the eider ducks at the end of the summer.

It will be a 2-day journey for Skipper Sr, his wife Irene, Saskia and me, there and back. I haven't spent much time with Petter since our intense meeting two summers before. Just occasional encounters when our paths cross between trips, the time for a meal or a drink or a walk together.

Now we have hours ahead of us and we speak late into the evening, talking about poetry and language and theatre and travelling and crossing the Hardangervidda – that big expanse in the middle of Norway my father and Uncle Otto loved so much. I remember my father telling me how they rode their bicycles the 200 km back to Oslo in a day.

The sea is calm and the boat is on autopilot. Every now and then Skipper Sr comes up to check something but we are speaking in Norwegian and he doesn't even attempt to join in. "So when are we going to walk or ski over the *vidda* together?" Petter teases. "Whenever you like," I respond. And then I change the subject, "Have you ever read or seen Aristophanes' play about the birds? It really reminds me of this place. There is material for a crazy adaptation."

"Why don't you do it?" he asks.

"You have the theatre experience," I reply, "I think we should do it together." We start leafing through the copy of Svalbard Birds that Skipper Sr keeps on board and fall into fits of laughter assigning bird avatars to the local bigwigs and other characters we know.

We hatch a plan for him to join the boat next year, so that he can see the north of Svalbard, and we can write together. I only half-believe in this plan – it doesn't sound realistic. But I haven't factored in Petter's capacity to throw himself into new projects once he gets an idea into his head.

In my memory, the light is golden when the boat glides away from the shore the next day. Hiawatha and Petter are on the beach in front of the house made of driftwood and Petter is playing a wooden flute. A variation on *So Long, Marianne*, one of the songs that haunted the bars of Longyearbyen the year the "Cohen in

Norwegian" album was released. I watch the figures of the two men blur into the background as we pick up speed. The melody fades behind the sound of the motor and the swish of water against the hull.

We stop briefly near the mouth of the fjord before raising the sails. I still have a photo. The Arctic sun is bright and I strip off for a swim. There are my head and bare shoulders, bobbing up between the white chunks of ice with sepia plateaus and pale blue sky in the background. Smooth rocks on the shore. What if a polar bear comes? Swimming in Svalbard brings me to the edge of myself. In every way. My whole body red and steaming when I emerge, my breathing fast. Irene throws me a towel.

We turn into the wind and head northwards again. ▨

Renata has homed in on a book about the birds of the area, "I didn't realize there were so many different birds here. No wonder you are obsessed with them…" She buys it, and is already sketching the different species by the evening. She is supposed to be the illustrator of the book we are writing together, but she has so much energy I am sure that if I don't write it, she will.

In fact she does have her own Viking story to tell, but that comes later.

That evening we decide to go for a walk with Jon up the Lars glacier and over towards the Troll Stone. We move slowly, looking at details, taking photographs. Near the back of town, a family of snow ptarmigans poses casually for us, all plump and fluffy and poultry-like, before we move up to the glacier.

The glacier is flat and easy to walk on, like many glaciers here – people unfamiliar with Svalbard are often surprised to find that rubber boots are the footwear of choice. But these flat glaciers have a dark and secretive side, and are marked at this time of year by beautiful and eerie twisting paths carved out by the meltwater that courses down the surface before disappearing into what seem to be bottomless caverns. I think of Tarjei Vesaas and his novel about a young girl, a newcomer with an unspoken burden, who disappears inside an ice formation in the dead of winter. And then I continue jumping casually over the rivulets and forget about the disquieting universe beneath.

And I recall the time I came over Lars glacier from the back, after exploring the abandoned Russian settlements and walking back up through Far Valley.

* SVALBARD BIRDS — A BASIC FIELD GUIDE
(BANGJORD, HAUGSKOTT & HAMMER, 2013)

Wastelands (1996)

Each valley is a way home
each valley is the barrel of a gun
kittiwakes cackle in the wings

Most of the guides I met the first year are back again.
Petter, the Artist, the Gentle Giant and the Geologist
are all here, although I miss Pixie who was not able to
make it. They all have some days off and have invited
me to join them on a walking trip to Grumant and Coles
Bay, two deserted Russian settlements. The Russians
have been industrious in setting up mining activities,
but quick to close up when the coal seams run low. The
only remaining towns are Barentsburg and Pyramiden, and
Pyramiden is only a couple of years away from closure.

 We meet at the port end of town and walk up the front
face of the plateau, behind the old coal cableway or
taubane – no longer in use, but its metallic grey silhouette against the bare mountain has become a local
icon. Behind it lie the wooden church and a graveyard
marked by a patch of bare white crosses. A scientific

team is awaiting permission to dig up the bodies of the men who died of the Spanish flu in 1918, but I am not around to witness the exhumation.

For some reason I have been designated as one of the gunbearers, and I bring up the rear of the group. The light is warm and oblique - we are already approaching the time of the first sunset.

A cluster of ptarmigans tumbles unexpectedly from behind a rock, waddling along with us as we start to walk upwards, before scattering into the charcoal sky. Our conversation is punctuated by long intervals of silence as we curve around beneath the shoulder of Nordenskiöldtoppen towards Bjørndalen. Different groups form and reform and we reform the world in our words and minds. The Geologist tells us about the unseen tellurian forces that have shunted fossils from sea beds to mountains and folded the rock like the soft drapery of a Roman sculpture.

The Artist has brought a thermometer. It is our temperature television. Our leisure time diversion. We turn it on each time we stop, and stare at its screen. Three degrees and falling.

Mud, wetness, reindeer over the plateau. We follow the tyre tracks that it seems some ancient people must have scraped into the fragile earth. We tread softly, but the blurred negatives of our soles remain imprinted in the topography.

More greyness and less light as we trudge up the other side of the valley. Crossing curious ice patches that appear to be deceptively small undiscovered glaciers. Ice bridges over miniature yawning chasms.

And then we take a rest to eat the reconstituted meat meal prepared with melted snow by the Artist, chef extraordinaire. Petter and I don't talk much. He and the other Swedes tell stories and sing songs in Swedish, mostly ditties by their national troubadour Cornelius Vreeswijk. His friend the Journalist has problems with the waterproofing of his boots so he takes them off for a while to try to dry his socks.

After walking for 10 hours or so we cut to the side, over an area of soft green earth, and arrive at the Russian cabin. By now it is breakfast time. What a way to break our fast – sitting outside at a table facing the ocean, like some sort of seaside picnic from more southern latitudes caught by a pre-impressionist, our faces washed out in the cloud-diluted light.

This is a quiet meal, we are all tired, and after eating we light the oven in the cabin and each bundle ourselves into our sleeping bags, sleeping until early evening (if the word evening has any meaning any more), almost uninterrupted except for the occasional zip-zip of overheated sleepers attempting to open over-efficient Arctic sleeping bags.

We are woken by unfamiliar voices, wondering in Norwegian about our identities and origins (are they Russian scientists? German tourists?). I am the only Norwegian of the bunch and only half at that, but I stir from my sleep and fill them in before they continue on their way. And who were they anyway?

It must be lunchtime by now, so the Artist prepares some soup before we set off for a side trip to Grumant. I sling the rifle over my shoulder.

He guides us towards the old Russian railway, where we leap from sleeper to sleeper in the wooden tunnel that used to connect the two settlements, choked with snow in parts. Sometimes shafts of light relieve the weight of the bulbless cords that dangle above us and the grafitti in Cyrillic, "the end is nigh".

When we come to the end of the line we continue on the trail that someone has marked out up the steep but green and grassy-looking hillside.

The tough part comes later. There is a river coming down through the moraine formations, so we scramble down a steep scree slope, cross a dubious ice bridge and almost don't make it up the other side, dislodging boulders that hurtle down. When we reach the top, there is a break in the grey that bathes us in golden-green light, and we lie flat for a while in the non-existent night.

Without words, we pick up our bodies again, and carry them down to the start of an old Russian road. The Artist knows a shortcut and the six of us slide down a narrow valley which spits us out at the bottom like shot from the bore of a gun.

And finally we arrive at Grumant, an uncanny realm of abandoned buildings, an atmosphere of overgrowth and decay in shades of blue and green, overtaken by gangs of gulls, each guarding its strip of windowsill territory.

We build a fire on the beach of stones, below the fluorescent green fertilized cliff faces and cook damper (damper - how far away am I from childhood camping trips in Australia?). And then we retrace our steps (how do we get back up that valley? we must have gone a different way) for more warm sleep in the Russian cabin.

Later, old tire tracks scraped into the earth lead us to Coles bay, another ghost town, even more ghostly than Grumant, a haunting place where chunks of 10-year-old bread and onion peel lie on tables, left over after the last meal. Strips of wallpaper are still intact in babies' rooms, beds unmade, tables still laid. They say the inhabitants left in a hurry all those years ago. Something I will hear later about Pyramiden – it seems it is part of the myth of the Russian ghost towns, that the entire population left overnight.

We, however, tarry before taking off, on our last shaky travelling legs. The next day, or should I say midday, we make our way up Far valley, in a sort of endless pilgrim's progress, punctuated by songs from Vreeswijk's *Felicia* suite, my soundtrack from that journey.

The last chocolate stop is in a small steep place with black earth and stones. We run down and up the other side of the dip, and then it's a final trek up towards the pass to Longyear glacier. I am at the front now, tilting my Voigtländer camera to make the angle of progression of our group walking in Indian file on the steep black slope look even steeper in the photos.

Towards the top, there are rivers and snow, and even wetter feet for those with poor shoes, and ice again, and a sign, "Do not pass here, dangerous crevasses!", signed the Governor.

The Journalist takes a photo of the sign (to be recovered as part of a roll of undeveloped film years later from the bottom of a glacier, I wonder, like the photos from explorer Andrée's fateful balloon trip many years before? I already imagine sarcastic comments from Norwegians, "It had to be a Swede"...).

But slowly, hopefully and ropelessly, we follow a set of footprints encrusted in the snow over the pass.

After which, acceleration, it's a race against time. It is almost 10 p.m., time for last orders for dinner at Huset - first one there takes the orders, so each of us memorizes the whole list: burgers, salad, chips... the Artist gets his second wind and disappears over the rise, followed by the Gentle Giant, the friend who would always tease me about being too full of energy, but the truth was that he was always strides ahead. The Geologist and I are somewhere in the middle, taking turns to roll down the hill a large chunk of petrified tree that we have come across in the moraine. Petter and the Journalist trail behind - they are still talking - but no one falls into a hole in the glacier.

The dark valley finally appears before us and we are back to the city of Longyear in the Sunday night-light. ▣

"Do you still have those photos?" Jon asks.

I must have them somewhere, but I haven't seen them for years. They are probably in that travel bag I've been lugging around unopened through my last three house moves.

Photographs – potent time machines, particularly the ones that go astray and are later unexpectedly discovered or rediscovered.

Faded negatives (1997)

There is a steady wind and I am at the helm as we sail back from Woodfjord. It felt so remote there that it is strange to think that we were actually closer to Longyearbyen as the crow flies than we are now. Had we sailed even further west, and down Wijdefjord, we could have ended up not far from Pyramiden. Yet land is so much more insurmountable than the ocean we sail on, at least at this time of year. Depending on the season and the means of transportation we relate to our environment in such different ways.

The time we sailed out to the ice pack my sense of space-time went into meltdown. Walking on pieces of frozen ocean, feeling it bobbing gently beneath my feet. How can this be the sea? How can *walking* be the way I move across this expanse? Closer to home, it strikes me whenever I am in Oslo in the winter and I put my skis back on for the first time to go out through Nordmarka forest. As I move through the trees, the landscape is familiar but alien. Not only does it look different to the woods I walk through in summertime, but I move at a different speed, and with a different kind of ease as I glide over marshes and lakes instead of having to walk around. It is the same place, and not the same place.

The Swedish polar explorer Andrée and his expedition members must have felt that so much more acutely as they struggled to make their way south on foot over the pack ice back to Svalbard in 1897, a 3-month journey to cover about the same distance as they had covered in just over two days in their hot air balloon.

The sea is calm as we sail past the north-west corner. I love this corner. Going through the passage between the islands and the mainland I feel shielded from the open sea to the north where there is nothing but water and ice between me and the North Pole.

Yesterday we realized we had the company of a whale. I was the first to notice the long dark back rising from the water on the port side. It was at least as long as the boat, and cruised right beside us for 10 minutes or so. We kept a steady and respectful course – it could have upended us if it had wanted. But without a breach or any other gesture it disappeared again.

Now we sail south towards Virgohamna, the bay on Danskøya island that saw the launch of Andrée's and various other mostly unsuccessful polar expeditions in the late 19th and early 20th centuries. The site itself represents layers of history, beginning with whalers back in the 1600s.

We tread softly, imagining it a hundred years ago as the explorers finally set off with a favourable southerly wind after the previous year's aborted attempt. Was it a reckless flight forward for Andrée, who could not have borne to lose face again? He had been told that the balloon was not airtight, that his plan for steering it was faulty. He hit problems from the start, releasing too much ballast, losing control and rising too quickly, only to then get weighed down by ice forming on the surface of the balloon. But there were the investors, the sponsors, the press, the national pride. The Arctic was, and still is, a place on the edge, at the final frontier, that invites adventure and fires up people's imaginations.

But what catches my imagination more than anything is the story of the photos.

After a carrier pigeon returned with a message on the 13th of July 1897, shortly after their departure, no further news of the expedition was ever received until the bodies of Andrée and his two companions, Strindberg and Frænkel, were found by chance in 1930 on Kvitøya, a remote island to the north-east of the archipelago.

Thirty-three years later. A generation. The find included extensive diaries, meteorological observations, drawings, and rolls of undeveloped film, some of which were in good enough condition to develop. A time machine, chronicling the last months of the lives of these three men, from the balloon that foundered on the ice, to the polar bears they slaughtered for food, to the flimsy boat they had been using to cross from one ice floe to another.

As we lift the anchor, I am happy to feel the northerly blowing, nudging us towards the south. ◼

We have picked up all the ingredients we need from the store downtown and are making Thai curry tonight with Jon and Psy-Girl. Is she the one who brings up the question of the different rhythms at which people live their lives? Or is it me, reflecting on Golden Boy's comment about Hiawatha, "I do in 10 minutes what it takes him a month to do…"? Or maybe it is Barenboim bubbling up in my mind with his theories about tempo.

"What if we are frequencies? Or rather our lives are frequencies, each with a certain shape and timbre?" Renata suggests. "And only some will fit together," I add, "whereas others might seem to for a time but then go out of sync." Petter used to wonder about the mystery of how two people could find harmony together as a couple. Not that he ever really tried to find it, it seems. Maybe it is unattainable. Is everything in life a compromise, where you converge towards an asymptote, approach a goal, but never quite reach it? Maybe the frequencies have to be divided up like the notes on a piano, never quite in perfect harmony but close enough if you are lucky. And are these frequencies subject to a kind of Doppler effect – expanding or contracting depending on where they are and where you are listening from?

My life until now seems to have been about overcoming fears, facing the dissonance rather than building on the harmonies. But they always linger: my fear of heights, my fear of speaking in front of other people, my fear of committing to a relationship. And then when I do overcome them, sometimes a concrete factor will pop up to prove that my fear was justified in the first place. Like falling into a crevasse.

I have another constant fear. "Does anyone else worry about being a fake?" I ask the group.

"You mean impostor syndrome?" replies Jon, "Weren't you talking about that the other day? They say it doesn't happen to men, but I suffer from it regularly. You have to have courage, project yourself into the role. Show grit in the face of adversity. There is a word for that in Finnish, *sisu*."

Sisu. I like that word.

One of the impostor scenarios that haunted me during my time in Svalbard was losing my Skipper overboard and not being a skilled enough sailor to save him. Fortunately I never had to test it, but one day we did lose the boat.

SOMETIMES MARIANNE SPENDS TOO
MUCH TIME ANALYSING HERSELF AND
NOT ACTUALLY DOING STUFF. GOOD
THING I'M HERE OR SHE'D NEVER GET
ANYTHING DONE.

The renegade yacht (1997)

Squeaking noise. A constant whine, its pitch oscillating behind the general sound of the wind buffeting the rolled sails. "Oh, so you have the same problem," says Skipper Jr to Skipper Sr. We have come over to join Saskia and Skipper Sr on their yacht for dinner.

"What problem?"

"The whining of the cables."

"Don't you know?" exclaims Saskia. "That's not the wind in the cables. It's not the boat at all. That is the mating call of the bearded seal. At certain times of year you can hear its underwater cry almost every day, vibrating through the hull."

We laugh in delight at this curious fact, and self-deprecation at our stupidity, and relief that we have one less problem to solve, and continue our meal of fresh fish. It is one of our first relaxed evenings in weeks after a rough crossing and days spent fixing various problems on our boat.

As we talk, the wind picks up. We can no longer hear any bearded seals seeking their soulmates. Skipper Jr glances out the porthole as he clears the table.

Merde!

Our yacht, which we had left moored a couple of hundred metres away before coming over for dinner, has come loose. The anchor has started dragging on the sea bed and the boat is now skimming across the bay unmanned.

I can't remember exactly what we do, everything went so fast that it has blurred in my memory, but it must be something like this: Skipper Jr and I quickly lower the Zodiac into the water and set off at top speed under the light rain, the wind beating against our ears, to catch up with our ghost ship before it hits a rock, an iceberg or the other side of the fjord.

I feel like a cowgirl with a mission to lasso a wild bull as we manage to subdue the wayward animal and bring it back to its anchorage by the port.

The sun has dipped low. It will start setting in a couple of weeks.

We skip dessert. ▨

It's getting late but not too late for a drink. "Let's go down to Kroa," says Jon. Renata and I are both tired, but it's one of my favourite bistros in town and Jon convinces us to join him. As we amble downtown I think back to the first walk the three of us took together when we had just arrived. It was only a couple of days earlier but it already seems like a universe ago. The sun is low and casts our long shadows across the valley. Our silhouettes blend in with the slats of the wooden houses arranged in colour-coordinated rows along the bottom of the hill as we speculate again about the future of this outpost.

Day 5
Other worlds

Wednesday – up early. Renata and I are taking a boat to Pyramiden, which was one of the two biggest Russian mining settlements. It remained active into the nineties but somehow I never got there before it closed operations in 1998. Now it is a ghost town that I am curious to discover.

And I will be back on the water again. My natural element. Or at least it was for a while. And I can't forget that this is how I first arrived in Longyearbyen.

Yet it feels strange to me to be a tourist on a boat. It doesn't feel quite right. I was always on the other side: the guide, the sailor, the passeur. I will have to come to terms with this new role.

We are not well-clothed to spend a lot of time on deck. The irony. I am not just a tourist, but also an ill-prepared tourist. Our movements become a choreography to keep warm, above, below, outside, in, and time on the bridge, eavesdropping on the captain's conversations. I'm happy that our presence is tolerated there. Back when I was working on the cruise liners, although I loved the company of the cruise director and the entertainers, I also liked to cross over to the other world of the ship, the world of the sailors and ship's officers. The bridge was one of my refuges.

IT'S REALLY COLD ON DECK. HOW DID WE NOT
COME BETTER PREPARED? MARIANNE SHOULD
KNOW BETTER.

Microcosms (1993)

Any ship is a microcosm. Cruise ships in particular consist of superimposed worlds in a strange coexistence – there is a society of people who make sure the ship is functioning, that it is on course, that it hits no rocks or icebergs. And then there is the society of people who are there to be entertained or to help people be entertained. It was the unfortunate conflation of the two that proved disastrous for the ship that ran aground many years later near Giglio island off the coast of Tuscany.

I am part of the entertainment. Sort of. Whereas the ship functions according to a caste system closely tied to nationality - from the Italian officers to the Israeli security staff and the Indian or Filipino waiters - I am the only one of my kind, so I manage to sidestep the social structure.

In my role as lecturer, I am on board to instruct and delight curious passengers with snippets of scientific information and tales of Norway. I wear a badge of credibility as a "true" Norwegian, but it is actually thanks to the fact that I am not fully Norwegian that I

can communicate with the passengers so well. I am between worlds, with one foot in France and the other in
Norway, seeing both from the inside and outside at the
same time.

Maybe because my father was a captain in the merchant
navy for many years, I have always felt at home on the
bridge of a ship. And perhaps because I am comfortable
moving between worlds, I am able to do so on this ship;
I can slip into spaces that are restricted for others.
Sometimes I sit up on the bridge with the officers in
the evenings as we head north, as the sun briefly nods at
the horizon before lifting its head again, and we talk a
bit, or are silent. Even the Italians sit quietly.

I think it is in Tromsø that the ice pilot comes on
board. He is a Norwegian expert who will come with us
for the leg all the way up to Svalbard and back. Also
somehow outside of the hierarchy. And we sit and speak
Norwegian and he shares his knowledge about the water,
and the coastline and the currents, about how it is that
ice forms and how it travels. The yearly freeze and melt
cycle, the difference between old ice and new ice, the
different communities of microorganisms that live in
and around the ice layers, and how the salt is squeezed
out of the ice crystals as the sea ice ages so it ends
up becoming freshwater.

These lessons about the Arctic ice remain with me
today. ▨

Renata is squatting, her back to the railing that keeps us all on deck, sketching the gaggles of tourists peering ahead. A French family admires her drawings of the different sea birds as we sail in towards Skansebukta and the remains of the gypsum mines there. I suddenly hear someone speaking Danish and it reminds me of Freddy, a friend lost not long before, my dear friend Liv's companion.

"Will you show our daughter how to draw?" the French parents ask, and Renata kindly obliges with a few tips.

I think back to when I used to draw. And how I met Renata because I wanted lessons. I even had my own modest cartoon series, but I never shared *The Lonesome Policeman* with more than a few friends. Now it is too much effort for me to draw – writing keeps me busy enough – but I miss it. When I was travelling and stopped to sketch something, clusters of curious strangers would often gather around to see what I was doing. Drawing has a certain immediate convening power that writing does not.

We all chat for a while. "Perhaps we will see you again in Paris?" says the father to Renata.

Back out and towards Pyramiden. Originally a Soviet utopia. We are accompanied by a young Norwegian guide, who mostly walks around with a gun looking out for bears, and a Russian who gives us the commentary. Pyramiden was a settlement for the elite, he tells us, "Only for the best of the best…" He has a slightly ironic undertone although his tour is enlightening, "Women had no kitchens so they were released from domestic slavery." He enumerates the different neighbourhoods: Paris, London, the Champs Elysées… They were well ahead of Longyearbyen and its new Beverly Hills quarter.

I haven't had that much contact with the Russians in Svalbard, but I did once stumble upon an unexpected opportunity for socialization. Unique actually, as there is – or at least used to be – little real contact up here between the Norwegians and the Russians. They meet, they communicate, but their lives are separate and very different, another example of worlds that coincide but remain fundamentally apart.

It was my second summer in Longyearbyen and I happened to run into Young Viking (in case you've forgotten, he's the French-speaking one from Toulouse, not one of the Vikings I ended up working with). "Hey, you're the guy who led me up Nordenskiöldtoppen last year," I exclaimed, surprised that he was back again.

"And what are you doing here?" he asked. We exchanged stories – he was about to take over the summer shift as interpreter once more – and he invited me to a dinner at the official interpreter's residence with some members of the Barentsburg Russian community the following Saturday.

"You mentioned you speak Russian, right?" he asked, and I nodded hesitantly. "Great, see you then, 5 p.m."

I was uncomfortable at first because my Russian credentials were poor but as the dinner progressed, with singing, dancing, vodka, singing, dancing and more vodka, accompanied by regular toasts and serenades by the accordion player, I soon felt at home. I wasn't sure whether the men were flirting or trying to strike mysterious deals or something else again, or maybe it was all tied together; the dark Georgian guy was particularly verbose but I couldn't quite get the drift. The women were mostly warm and smiling and patient with my faltering Russian. The official interpreter it turned out used to go to school with my brother. More strange connections.

Eating and dancing. I like the way the Russians can throw a party at any time of day. Of course the 24-hour daylight helps.

But there will be no parties here at Pyramiden today. "Watch out for bears," our Norwegian guide warns. "There was one sighted near here last week." The surroundings look pretty calm, but you really never can know. I came face to face with one only on one occasion.

THE ONLY POLAR BEARS I SAW DURING
MY STAY WERE EITHER STUFFED OR
IMAGES IN BOOKS OR ON POSTCARDS.

This stuffed one is at the airport.

This one is at the
entrance to the main
shop, Svalbardbutikken.

The mythical beast (1997)

We have come round the north-west corner and are entering Woodfjord. This is supposed to be bear territory. As usual, I scan the horizon when we arrive, but I see nothing.

Water on the yacht is running low and I am in desperate need of a shower. The weather is calm and we anchor without incident. I decide to go ashore and wash in a stream. As I climb into the Zodiac everyone jokes, "Watch out for bears."

I leave the Zodiac on the beach and walk up to the stream. I lay my rifle on the ground and peel off my layers, one by one. I have a quick pee before I plunge into the glacial meltwater, which is just a couple of degrees above freezing. The icy cold water turns my whole naked body numb. I wash my hair and can feel my scalp turn hard, clamping my skull like cold metal. I glance at the suds from my bar of soap in the otherwise crystal-clear stream and feel a pang of guilt. Hopefully not too many people will follow my example. The earth is so fragile here that even footprints last for years, and tyre tracks last forever. I console myself with the thought that I am probably the first and last person to ever want to carry out their toilette in this particular place.

My fingers are so stiff from the cold that I can hardly get my clothes back on. If a bear comes now, I think, I wouldn't even be able to get my deadened fingers around the trigger of my gun.

But there is no movement on this bare hill. I walk back down to the beach, my hair almost steaming now that my scalp has come back to life. Before climbing into the Zodiac and starting back to the yacht, I sit for a while on the beach looking out at the water. It is so quiet here. So big. And I am so small. My life in the city is so far away, almost meaningless.

I am the first up the next morning. Up on the hill, by the stream, sniffing the ground, is a large white beast. This is the first live polar bear I have seen since childhood excursions to the zoo.

It occurs to me that he knows me now too. Knows my smell, at least the smell of my urine. Or is it a she? We set sail that day without disembarking, and our course is accompanied by a mother bear and her cub, swimming along the coastline.

When we reach our next anchorage, everyone is restless. They haven't left the boat in two days. We have only a few square metres to share and arguments ignite easily. We decide to go ashore, although the passengers on our companion boat stay on board.

The landscape on this small island is not the most beautiful. It is uneven brown hilly terrain. Our Zodiac is so small I have to take the passengers over in two trips. We have only crossed a few muddy hillocks when we see the white of a bear in stark contrast to the brown background. He looks at us. We look at him. "Can we take photos?" someone asks. The bear is very close.

"No, I think we should focus on getting back to the boat."

Someone tells me that he has risen up onto his hind legs, but I am already steering everyone in the other direction. I am hoping that he doesn't cut us off on the way back to the Zodiac or get there first - I've heard that bears love getting their claws into rubber. I'm also thinking about the fact that the Zodiac won't hold everyone. I try calling both boats with the walkie-talkie so that someone can come and help bring back the group. But the walkie-talkie is not working.

We reach the beach without seeing the bear again. After some thought about how to get everyone back in the best way - reminiscent of those mental puzzles where you have to get both the fox and the hen over the river without the hen getting eaten - it turns out that someone else knows how to drive a Zodiac. So he takes the first group back as I wait with the others, gun at the ready.

Soon we are all on board, the passengers chattering excitedly ("She wouldn't let us take photos!"). We set sail - we will be heading homewards again now. ▨

But no bears materialize today. Instead we photograph the painted image that graces the peeling sign that used to announce the presence of the coal company, Arktikugol, and the bust of Lenin planted on a column of grey concrete, facing out towards the fjord.

We wander through the abandoned buildings where people used to live, eat and play after long days in the mines. I take snaps of Renata striking poses in the dance practice room and we speculate about the content of the reams of film that have spilled out across the floor in the cinema. There is even a swimming pool which has lain many years empty. Above us looms the triangular peak that gave this town its name.

We buy postcards at a small shop that has been set up in the makeshift hotel. I am told that about three people live here to maintain the tourist operations and I ask whether it's possible to rent a room. This could be a place for me to work on my book while practising my Russian, I speculate. Impossible, I am told.

We board the boat once more, a sleepy ride back. We stop briefly in front of a nearby glacier and the sun comes out, but there is no calving today, just a few seals lazing on their sunbeds of ice.

And then past the natural formations of Tempelfjord, the stone parapets rising like organ pipes above us. Last time I came to Tempelfjord was by Zodiac.

THE PASSENGERS TRY TO CAPTURE A LAST SHOT
OF PYRAMIDEN BEFORE IT FADES INTO THE
BACKGROUND LIKE A GHOST.

Unmoored (1997)

Waiting. Waiting again in this small airport. The German and I chat a little. His smile is always warm and crinkly as he tells some story, or even when he is complaining about local politics. He is intrinsically connected to this airport in my memory, in my mind. Forever giving me a lift there or back, even long after I stopped working for him.

There is always a Kvikk Lunsj chocolate bar or two in the middle of the front seat of his orange van. Kvikk Lunsj is Norway's answer to Kit Kat - but decades of effective marketing have associated it with nature and the outdoors and so it stands for wholesomeness, no guilt. He pulls one out of his pocket now and we share it as we wait for the plane which is running a bit late.

He and Petter greet each other first. Bear hug. And then Petter and I embrace cautiously. There has never been anything official between us but the German looks away politely.

This year Petter is joining me to work on the boat. We have been writing each other letters throughout the winter and spring, brimming with plans and ideas.

But this is pre-mobile phones, so he doesn't know Anna Karenina was grounded yesterday for not complying with safety regulations, following the breakdown of the depth sounder and radar. I fill him in during the ride to town. I am not concerned. I see before us walks and discoveries while this is sorted out. And we still can write together, work on that play. But he gets a strange look in his eyes as I explain the situation and I feel uneasy. To make matters worse, his luggage with all his gear got left behind when he changed flights in Oslo.

I can't remember who comes to pick us up in the Zodiac. I think it must have been Saskia. Both skippers are there, Skipper Sr's wife Irene as well, and their small daughter. We eat dinner together and catch up. The little girl takes to Petter and sits happily on his lap, giggling as he teases her. And then the hour gets late. Everyone else has returned to their boat or is in bed.

He smells like nutmeg, just like I remember. I even used to keep a nutmeg kernel among my things that I would pull out sometimes when he had faded in my mind. But tonight there is too much distance between us, despite the intense exchange of letters that seemed to promise otherwise. We will have to learn each other all over again. I cannot remember which cabin we sleep in that night. For some reason in my mind's eye we are in my cot in the dining area, smack in the middle of the boat, but that can't be right. What I do remember clearly is that something feels out of kilter, as though he is tuned to a different frequency. I try to push that uncomfortable thought out of my mind, but it only serves to fix it there in the dark.

The original plan had been to sail up around the northern areas for two weeks, and then to help sail the boat back to the mainland, crossing the Barents Sea. But on a stationary vessel he is soon bored, a prisoner who makes no effort to escape. I am sure he could be released from his contract – I suggest he look for work with one of the other tour operators. He knows plenty of people. I take the Zodiac over to the port each day to meet friends and walk away the solitude. But he mostly stays on board and broods. And his gear has still not turned up. I call the airline each day on his behalf.

Even when he does come out socializing is difficult. He avoids the German, maybe embarrassed that he has somehow become trapped by this situation. When we go to Huset together to eat, our combined bad energy chases away anyone who might have joined us for a bite to eat. Until the alcohol starts flowing and he is again the centre of attention in the miners' bar and the women cluster around him like moths. And really I don't want to be his prison warden, I could leave him there to live his own life, that might be better for everyone. But we have only one Zodiac and we are sharing the same living space, and I feel somehow responsible. And this is a small town and there is an element of fear of losing face by association if he does something crazy or stupid. And I don't have anyone else in my life at this time and nor does he, that I know of, so this is the closest we ever become to being anything like a couple. So I drag him away from the miners' bar in the early hours of the morning.

Petter becomes increasingly insufferable, and I snap back, losing my patience.

But there are brief breaks in the clouds between us. One day remains encapsulated for me in a photo. A Swede in borrowed white rubber boots that look like they come from a house and garden store, wearing one of my jackets, his dark hair tied back in a ponytail. A bucket, a rifle, a thermos of tea and a packet of biscuits. The Zodiac on the beach. The giant organ pipes of Tempelfjord in the distance. The sky a soft steely grey.

Together with Saskia, we have rented out the Zodiac; it's a more powerful model than the one we have on board the yacht for taking passengers ashore. The tension is slowly dissipating as we set out to explore a part of Isfjord that none of us has been to before. We don bright orange survival suits, pack the rifle and provisions into waterproof bags and set off across the fjord, the cold wind teasing colour into our cheeks as we gain speed. When we reach the other side, we follow the shoreline for a while before finding a place to disembark and explore.

Saskia says she is going to search for blue stones and leaves us on the beach. "Watch out for bears!" Our leitmotiv. But after a few minutes we begin to fret. What if a bear really does appear from somewhere? She is unarmed and out of sight now.

And then Petter starts to sing, *Saskia had a name with a ring to it*, the Swedish troubadour Vreeswijk's story of the cross-eyed girl. I don't know the words but I join in where the lyrics repeat and the sound rings out among the rocks. We are willing Saskia to return, and then there she is, smiling to the strains of the slow three-step tune, although she can't understand the words, holding out the blue stones that she has somehow managed to find.

And we sip hot sweet tea and eat biscuits and the tension has completely gone, for now. We go for a walk together and then pack up our temporary camp. We bundle into the boat, rev the engine and the Zodiac lifts its nose from the water as we turn its head for home. There is no other boat in sight. No other people. No animals except for the birds. Fulmars and storm petrels skimming the waves, tracing graceful arcs through the leaden sky, accompanying our brief voyage.

A week later Petter has found himself a room in town and moved off the boat. His luggage has finally arrived and he has some part-time work lined up. "I need space," he tells me. "I want to write. Maybe finally work on something new."

"We can meet up," I suggest. "Do you still want to work on that adaptation of *The Birds*? Aristophanes I mean?" Not the other one, even though we are both fans of the Norwegian author Tarjei Vesaas and his novel *Fuglane*.

"Sure, we can meet up," he replies. "But I don't really want to work with you right now. You can keep that project for yourself." I feel somehow betrayed, by this more than anything else. I thought we had found a project to work on together. Connecting my creativity to his, anchoring myself to his drive. I'm sure he knows I can't work alone, that I founder and lose my nerve, my focus. "Ok," is all I say. He doesn't like to be anchored. ▧

On the boat I flip through *Hilsen fra Svalbard* ("Greetings from Svalbard"), a book made up of postcards sent by early visitors to the archipelago, recounting the history of the islands through images born of a slowly developing tourism industry, and the words that the travellers chose to tell their friends and families about their adventures.

I search for it later but cannot find it in any bookshops or online, despite my best efforts. It is tantalizingly similar and yet very different to the book I am trying to write, my play cum not-sure-what, my letters from the Arctic, which I originally saw as a series of postcards, my version of your *Letters from Iceland*.

And Renata and I chat to the Norwegian guide, about his love of Svalbard, his passion for the wilderness. He is young but has already caught the Arctic bug and keeps coming back. He takes his responsibility as a guide very seriously. He is probably the same age I was when I first came here. It is strange to think that he would have been born around that time, but now he is the expert, the local, and I submit to his guidance and knowledge. This is not the same world for me, in so many ways.

But he is curious about my stories too. I tell him about the time I sailed up to the ice edge – he hasn't been that far north yet. The ice is receding further each year, so I hope he makes it.

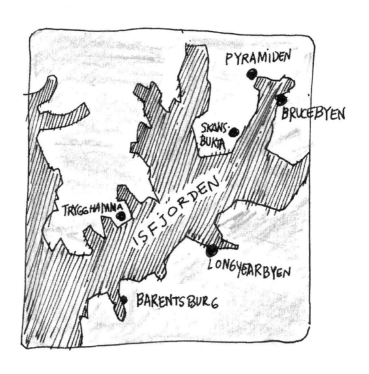

The ice pack (1996)

"We don't mind eating the miles," say the sailors from Brittany we have on board. They want to see the sea ice. Walk on the ocean.

Skipper Sr grunts. He doesn't want to promise anything. Getting to the edge of the ice pack can be tricky. It isn't necessarily open sea and then an uninterrupted sheet of ice. The edges crack and pieces of different sizes break away, and then run up against each other again, depending on the wind and currents. Sailing there can mean seeking a path through narrow channels between moving islands. Or trying to escape the small blocks that can come crowding around the boat and sometimes even freeze together again. When the ice is tricky, someone climbs up onto the mast to see the patterns and movement, and points out to the crew the best way to go.

But we decide we will try to reach the summer ice edge, up at around 80° north. A place where you can stand and mull over the fact that you could possibly walk from there all the way to the pole. Not that any of us will ever do that. That is the realm of intrepid explorers like Norway's national hero, Fridtjof Nansen, whose life my father used to like telling me about.

The Vikings have given me time off to go on this trip, and Blond Viking drops me down to the wharf in the early hours of the morning. We leave Longyearbyen at about 5 a.m., heading out of Isfjord, named for the ice that collects in it – although there is none here now. We pass Ymerbukta, a bay marked by its low rounded glacier, and on the other side Grønfjord, where dinosaur footprints were found. Giant tracks of prehistoric creatures caught there in the cliff, as though they just walked off into the sky one day.

And then the mountain between Ymerbukta and Trygghamna, with its folds of old rock, metamorphosed by the mysterious pressures of tectonic plates. It is like a giant toaster with endless rows of bread slices caught just as they popped up millennia ago.

There is a place with walruses too. I don't remember exactly where. We are walking along a beach and suddenly they are there. Almost blending in with the large stones except for the stench rising from their leathery salt-encrusted bodies – they must be the smelliest animals in the Arctic. They are piled on top of each other, not doing much, occasionally wiggling themselves into a more comfortable position. We tiptoe around them respectfully and then make our way back to the boat.

Our route leads us past coasts that I haven't seen before, on either side – we set our course through the sound, Forlandsundet. The nature of this place settles within me, the low grey cloud, the alternation of black, white and dark grey of rock, ice and cloud. An abstraction that is real. Like a painting by Kåre Tveter.

Punctuated by the flight of kittiwakes and fulmars. There is a swell, nothing big, but it brings on my first seasickness, running up on deck to return my lunchtime soup to the sea. I blame my middle brother, my childhood mentor who still holds sway over my beliefs – it is only after he told me one day that anyone can get seasick that I realized that it could happen to me too.

And then we are eating the miles, heading north. We are lucky, the wind is with us, and we decide to go with it.

We stop only once before we are out of the sound. We all feel the need to stretch our legs. In my memory it is a grassy hill, but of course it isn't. The only truly grassy place in Svalbard is at Pyramiden. There they imported grass from Siberia and it still graces the avenues of what is left of the town now that the mining operations have closed down.

But this place carries no sign of human presence. Just a few birds that swoop up from the water, and perhaps the trace of an Arctic fox in the air. I am sniffing a bit and my friend the skinny Breton offers me the other half of a used serviette he had taken from the lunch table. We agree that sailing together in the Arctic lends us enough intimacy to blow our noses on the same paper napkin.

Further north, we anchor at the place where Swedish explorer Andrée departed for his ambitious and ill-fated attempt to reach the North Pole in a hot-air balloon, almost a century ago. This northern corner of Svalbard is also haunted by a whalers' cemetery, mounds of stones on one of the islands. And the old houses and blubber ovens of these 17th century adventurers who came looking for adventure, and maybe an escape from misery. The trace of man in this region is superficial, and yet so lasting, the smallest signs preserved from erasure by the cold.

The whalers whittled down the whale population until there was no fortune left to make, and then they left too. Now the whales are back.

As we approach the 80th parallel the wind drops, and we have the motor running for the last few nautical miles. Everything is so still that it is easy to glide in through the floating ice when we reach the edge. It is a silent magic place of dark canals and rising mist, like something out of a Narnia book, between worlds. It seems as though the place itself muffles our speech, but perhaps we are the ones who lower our voices.

Skipper Sr brings the nose of the boat right up to the edge and we disembark from the front. His wife Irene is with us on this trip, and their one-year-old daughter. Someone passes her down from the boat and she plays happily in the snow covering the ice. Perhaps, apart from the Inuit, she is the youngest person on this planet ever to have walked on the Arctic ice pack?

As we touch the strange floating platform a rush of excitement seems to break through our quiet awe and the skinny Breton and I link arms to dance a waltz, our movements displacing ever so slightly the ice on the water below and making us heady. The same strange sensation of the world moving under my feet will come back to me briefly a few years later, as I steady my feet on one of the floating islands on lake Titicaca, in the highlands between Peru and Bolivia, but those are completely human-made, woven from the reeds of the lake.

The ice creaks slowly and strangely. We shouldn't stay too long in this place. The weather could change. We climb back on board and sail away from the hushed frozen ocean, our faces turned south.

As we enter Isfjord again, we choose to sail along the southern edge of the fjord and stop in Barentsburg before returning to Longyearbyen. But we have been away from civilization for days and don't know what has happened in our absence. Vnukova flight 2801, a Russian Tupolev bringing back a shift of miners and their families from holidays back home, had miscalculated its approach and crashed into Opera mountain, a couple of kilometres from the airport. There were no survivors. Everyone in town had friends and relatives on board. Faces are streaked with tears and it is not the right time for us to be here.

As we leave, I see a monument to the sailors of a boat that went down years before between Murmansk and Barentsburg. I had never noticed this monument before – it seems like a fold in time. ▨

We disembark. The town is as calm as the sea on this quiet afternoon.

My phone reconnects to the network and I see that Eli has left a message, "I've organized for you both to stay at my friend Gøril's place when you come back through Oslo! She's away at the moment. Oh, and we're going to have breakfast together on Saturday, ok?"

"There will be a surprise guest there who knows you both from Paris," she adds. Who could that be? Renata and I rack our brains.

We catch the bus back up to Nybyen, where we pause briefly to collect our bicycles and ride back down to Hiawatha's place as we had agreed the day before.

Renata will be working on his logo. I am marginally involved as a translator, refraining myself from playing my usual workplace role as moderator between designers and clients. Hiawatha is difficult and wants an exact rendition of the eider duck. He cannot find the right drawings or photos to use as a basis.

"It is like when you see a portrait of a friend – and that is not my friend, I can see it…" he judges of Renata's first attempt. So he decides to go out and look for some real eiders. "You come too," he gestures to me.

"Don't spend too long looking," says Renata, "If you can't find them easily, just come back…"

We hop in the car and drive first to the small point nearby where Hiawatha likes to fish. Nothing. We jump back in the pickup and drive to the shore by the campsite. Nothing there either. "How strange," he mutters. So we head further in towards Longyearbyen, but there is no sign of the eiders there, just a few shy sandpipers scurrying along the shore. (This is not a wild goose chase… or is it?) Finally we give up, but as we drive back towards the house we see them: two families, one on the beach, one bobbing up and down in the shallows. We leap out. "Don't walk so fast, you'll scare them!" So I slow my pace to dead slow, while he hides behind an object on the beach and sneaks out to take a few photos of his dear friends. Then back in the car.

I MADE SOME SKETCHES FOR HIAWATHA'S EIDERDOWN
BUSINESS BUT I'M NOT SURE HE EVER USED THEM.
I'M KEEPING AN EYE OUT FOR TOP DOWN.

Renata glances up from her sketchbook as we enter. Her eyes tell me we've been away for a while and I apologize. "It's ok," she says. In the end we don't even use the photos. She has moved ahead in her drawing, and it's pretty good.

Hiawatha guides her in getting the lines of the beak just right. Then there are questions of colour and shading. So in the end it takes hours. While they work, I skim the bookshelves. Hiawatha's mother was an artist and I sit for a long time with the book filled with the powerful lines and muted colours of her landscapes. In the early hours of the morning, he offers to put our bicycles in the pickup and drive us back up to Nybyen. I would have ridden back but Renata is happy to accept. Actually, I am also happy to accept.

Cross-fade to the kitchen. Jon is still up. He is sitting chatting to the Norwegian Country Counter. He offers us his leftovers and we sit down and talk awhile. How is the play going? Even Country Counter has joined the support group, encouraging me get this thing done.

"I got a bit stuck on the last part," I respond, "where the original moves on from the interactions between humans and the birds and starts to involve the Greek gods. I wasn't sure what to do about the gods. Who are our gods?

"First I thought about using the Norse gods. And then I realized: Our modern-day gods reach us via the virtual worlds that we navigate through every day. They connect us remotely to real places and objects too – via telecommunications and worldwide delivery services for example. Some of these gods are more benevolent than others. Many are driven by notions of profit and power. We pray to them, sacrifice to them, and open ourselves to their control and all-seeing gaze. Some of us are enslaved to them, and almost all of us depend on them. These forces affect the Arctic too."

"Now the web and the applications that feed on it are shaping our lives," comments Renata. "They are manipulating our minds. Or

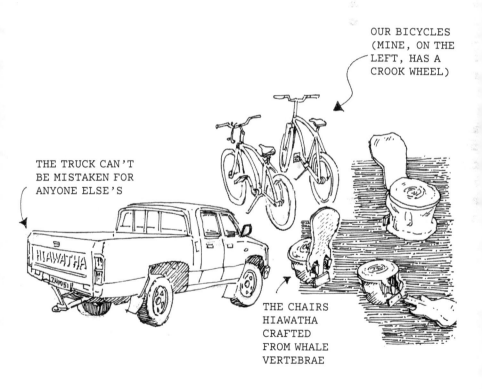

OUR BICYCLES
(MINE, ON THE
LEFT, HAS A
CROOK WHEEL)

THE TRUCK CAN'T
BE MISTAKEN FOR
ANYONE ELSE'S

HIAWATHA

ZNM051

THE CHAIRS
HIAWATHA
CRAFTED
FROM WHALE
VERTEBRAE

WE ENDED UP STAYING REALLY LATE, SO WE ACCEPTED
HIAWATHA'S OFFER TO GIVE US A RIDE BACK UP TO
NYBYEN.

maybe I should say 'your minds'," she adds with a smile, "seeing as I don't even own a mobile phone."

"Who says you're immune because you don't have a phone?" I object.

"But there are also true visionaries and dreamers," adds Jon, "people who use technology to share knowledge for the common good. Look at the open software and collaborative research movements. Maybe we're seeing the emergence of a hivemind?"

"But can we trust the people involved?" Renata cuts in. "Or will they succumb to their own power games?"

Maybe together we can come up with some answers, I think, maybe we are part of a greater wisdom, even if we don't realize it. And maybe the clumsy images that I can call up with my small voice have a part to play.

Day 6
Connections

Thursday we wake to beautiful clear skies. The sun has gotten visibly lower, and the town fills with golden light from all angles. There is not much time left before we are due to fly out and there are still people I am trying to track down. I try yet another number for the German. No luck. And then I try Blond Viking, whose number Tom the Bike has managed to dig up for me.

At first Blond Viking doesn't understand who I am on the phone, and I'm still not quite sure when the penny drops... "Your Norwegian is still really good," he says generically. When things have apparently clicked, he asks me what my plans are. "Flexible," I say. "Don't move," he replies, "I'll pick you up in five minutes."

And there he is. Short grey hair now, but let's call him Blond Viking anyway. He still has the same tender creases around his eyes when he smiles. I remember how he called me stubborn and clever – or was it twisted and mixed up? – but he probably wouldn't recall that now.

"Let's have lunch," he suggests, pointing to his truck. "Jump in." It's only 11.30 but I can eat at any time of day. "Do you mind if I bring my Peruvian friend?" He raises his eyebrows inquisitively, wondering whether I have brought a lover, maybe someone I told him about years ago. But figures it's not when Renata walks out and I introduce them.

In some ways it is as though no time has passed since we last met. He shows the same easy-going camaraderie. But then again, he is like this with everyone. One of the reasons why he is well-loved within the community. The three of us pile into the front seat of his pick-up and he takes us down to the Polar Institute where he works now. Not far from where I saw him step out of a truck a couple of decades earlier, the seed of my Longyearbyen guiding career. He gives us a tour of the institute, showing us all the equipment and machinery before buying us lunch at the cafeteria.

As we speak I start to sense the full weight of the years. We have not exchanged a word since I was last in Svalbard and life has marked us in different ways. Did I really use to share both an office and a sleeping space with this person? I have witnessed none of the life-changing events he has been through in the meantime, and he knows nothing of mine.

"I didn't know you had been sick." I don't know what to say.

"Yeah, all these years of polar night, can't be good for you..." he replies with his signature touch of irony. I do recognize him, I tell myself. He changes the subject.

"I've gotten involved in politics. I reckon Longyearbyen could be a model town. What other place is there like it? Practically no crime, even though everybody carries a gun. No drugs, maybe just a bit too much drinking on the weekends. No unemployment. A mix of nationalities, yet harmonious. And it could be even better.

"We could eliminate so much waste, make things much more eco-friendly... It would be great for everyone up here. And an example to follow for the rest of the world. Some people think I'm misguided or naïve but I actually got 15 percent of votes in the last elections."

He almost sounds like one of the characters in *The Birds*, selling utopia, although he is speaking in earnest.

Renata is sketching and only jumps into the conversation now and again. She has a presence that she can change the focus control on, where she voluntarily blurs herself into the edge of your field of vision by being very still, and then comes back sharp and strong when she re-engages in the conversation. Like now.

BLOND VIKING

FOR SOME REASON I
WAS EXPECTING BLOND
VIKING TO HAVE LONG
HAIR. AND TO BE BLOND.
AND TO LOOK WILD AND
ADVENTUROUS. IT TURNS
OUT HE HAS SHORT-
CROPPED GREY HAIR
AND IS AN ASPIRING
POLITICIAN.

People can be adverse to change. This
could be a model town if we really tried,
ecological, responsible...

"But do you really think you can introduce a sustainable model up here when all the food is flown in from the continent? When apartments have to be heated year round?"

Blond Viking has some answers but she is not satisfied. And at a certain point she reminds me about our next appointment. Keeping tabs on me again. "Shouldn't we get going? Saskia will be waiting for us at the quay."

It was Hiawatha who told me when I would be able to find Saskia – he has memorized the schedules of all the boats that come out and in.

We take our leave, and promise to write, knowing as we promise that we probably won't. And Blond Viking will blur again and return to my reimagined past.

Now it is Saskia coming into the foreground. We are real friends surely? Or we were. We sailed together. Co-wrote poetry. Borrowed each other's sleeping bags. She writes to me at least once a year although I am not always so good at keeping up. It has been a few years now since I have seen her in person, but we have managed to meet up sporadically, in the off season between polar summers, when she is neither in Svalbard nor the Antarctic.

She is not waiting at the quay, so we stand on the shore and wave. She has being watching out for us and zips over in the Zodiac.

"Saskia!" We hug. It is strange to meet here, back on a boat together. It's not the one I used to work on, but I have been on it before. I was the informal translator when Skipper Sr bought it, just after I stopped sailing. And Saskia took over full time when I left.

I introduce Renata – they have heard about each other before, but never crossed paths. Renata is relieved to be speaking French again after days of struggling in English (which is her fourth language after Spanish, French and Cantonese).

Saskia pours tea and offers us slices of a cake that she has made, a Norwegian recipe that a friend handed on to her. Years ago she passed the recipe on to me together with the secret for keeping it for months without it going stale or mouldy. I like the name of this cake, "house friend", but I'm not sure whether she made it up or something got lost in translation. Another Norwegian friend tells me it's called a *skuffekake*, or cake you can keep in the drawer.

Many of the things from the old boat were handed over, like when moving house, and I recognize the mugs and plates that she hands us. On the shelf in the kitchen area I spot a familiar folder, a folder of recipes. The "house friend" and many others – there are even some I wrote down myself. Seeing my handwriting makes me shiver, in a time travel kind of way. I wasn't ready to come face to face with myself. So strange that a part of me is still here, in such a concrete and immediate way, bound up in these kitchen fragments.

I come across a stained sheet of paper with the recipe for chocolate charlotte. That was one of Skipper Jr's recipes – he used to sing and recite sad poems about drowned sailors when making it, and it became one of my desserts. I still make it today.

WE STAND AND WAVE FROM THE SHORE, HOPING THAT
SASKIA WILL SEE US.

At the edge (1997)

The idea was to have a swish meal to celebrate the 14th of July, French national day. We stopped earlier in the day for a walk - in my memory it was on an island, perhaps Danskøya, although now I am not so sure - before continuing north.

The wind is strong and the sea choppy. No one is hungry. In fact no one is to be seen except for Skipper Jr and me.

I work on a charlotte, melting the chocolate squares and butter into a smooth mixture on the stove that I have released from its fixture so that it can swing and remain horizontal, whatever the angle of the boat. I will fasten it later when we anchor. I have become very careful about my cooking on board ever since the cod episode, when I had forgotten to close the catch again and the whole baked cod swung out, sailing through the air as though it had briefly grown wings before flopping sadly onto the floor.

I knock on a few doors and quiz the passengers on whether they would rather eat as we sail - i.e. at a reasonable hour - or when we arrive at anchor.

Pasty faces emerge briefly from the dim cabins to confirm their preference for the second option.

We finally arrive at our destination for the day, together with our sister vessel, which has Skipper Sr on board. A strong wind is blowing and it is hard to anchor, especially as our depth sounder is no longer working. It can't have been night – it is still summer – but I remember it as being dark; maybe it was overcast, and the sun was probably at its lowest in the 24-hour cycle. Maybe it was tucked behind the mountains already.

The chain of events is like a reel being fast-forwarded in fits and starts. Standing on the deck, manoeuvering as Skipper Jr throws down a weighted line to check the depth as they used to do in the olden days. The wind pushing us towards the rocks, us struggling to get the anchor down fast enough.

Finally, finally we are at anchor. I climb back down into the boat to get dinner onto the table. It is nearly midnight.

Dinner will be *confit de canard* – duck meat that has been cured and preserved in its own fat, a French specialty. It goes well with couscous and the whole meal can be prepared in five minutes and still look swish. One of the tricks I learned from Saskia. At times like these it is better to avoid boiled potatoes, which can quickly turn into mash if a manoeuvre takes too long.

We are seated, taking our first bites, when we hear disquieting scraping sounds. Skipper Jr goes up to check and shouts for me to come up. The anchor has come loose and is dragging along the sandy bottom littered with stones – we are dangerously close to the rocks.

We begin the manoeuvres yet again. By the time we get down, dinner is cold. Everyone has been waiting for us to return before starting to eat. It is Bastille day after all. One of our passengers has a strange look on his face. His eyes are glazed over and there is something scary about this look, as though he is possessed by an evil spirit.

I'd seen this look earlier. Just a glimpse of it as it crossed his face for an instant just before lunch. Uncanny. I thought briefly about it and then moved on.

He hardly responds to our questions now and his cabin mate guides him back to his cabin to lie down. But we are worried and decide to check his toiletries for medicines.

Perhaps he has overdosed on seasickness tablets?

We find insulin. Pause. He is a diabetic and we didn't know. We look at him and realize he is on the verge of coma. He probably needs sugar, but we are not quite certain. If we get it wrong he will die. If we don't do anything at all, he will certainly die. We are many sea miles away from the closest thing to civilization. There is not even a satellite connection here for what that would be worth at this point.

We call the other boat and find out that one of their passengers is a nurse. She speeds over to us on the Zodiac. In the meantime we show him a lump of sugar. Given the circumstances, we are almost sure this is what he needs. We think we detect a sign of acquiescence in his almost immobile face, and the nurse, who has now arrived, tells us to go ahead. As the sugar melts on his tongue, his eyes begin to clear and his face slowly returns to normal. It is magic.

The anchor is dragging again. Skipper Jr and I run up, leaving our passenger in the hands of the nurse. I can't remember actually eating that evening, but I suppose we did eventually. ∎

"So what have you been up to these past few years?" I ask.

And Saskia tells us how she overwintered one year, and learned how to mush dogs, but living through the months of cold and darkness once was enough for her. She prefers going to the Antarctic for the southern daylight when it's winter in the northern hemisphere. Her family and friends think she's a bit crazy, working on a boat year in year out. She still loves it, but is starting to feel the pressure to do something different, maybe even settle down, have kids. She tells me about Skipper Sr's daughters, all grown up and sophisticated now. "I might take a break soon," she says. And adds teasingly, but actually half-serious, "Feel like getting your old job back?"

A yawning chasm opens up, like the one in that house in Danielewski's *House of Leaves*. A space where there isn't really room for a space in my mental architecture. Just like that, I could pick up where I left off. I had handed everything over to Saskia 17 years ago, and now she could in turn hand it back to me, just like that?

Renata comments that there seems to be a small Zodiac approaching. We climb up on deck and greet the visitors. They are friends of Saskia's who have just come into harbour, travelling with a scientific expedition on another vessel. One of them mentions that the Anthropologist is on board as well. The man who first hired me to work on the cruise ships, and then sent me up the following year to try to start a guiding company. Strange, for some reason I thought that he had vanished from the whole Arctic scene. I haven't seen him since that time he came up to research the trappers, 20 years ago.

Lost in translation (1994)

The Anthropologist has come in on one of the cruise ships, where he is working as a lecturer, and is here in Longyearbyen for a couple of days. He has given up the idea of the guiding company for this year at least, and seems relieved that I have found other things to keep me busy. And he has a new activity for me: interpreter. He wants to interview a trapper who is in town, and although I don't speak Italian his English is good, so we will make do with that. He has come armed with a letter from the dean of his university and boundless enthusiasm for the life of the trapper.

We begin the evening in the Trapper's apartment in Longyearbyen, where he stays when he is not in his cabin up north. The walls are adorned with photos of his trapping and hunting activities: skinning seals on the beach, hanging meat up to dry on a giant rack.

He is the first trapper I meet in Svalbard, this is before I get to know Hiawatha. I tell him about my uncle's life as a trapper years before in north-east Greenland, in between translating for the Anthropologist, who is full of superlatives and praise for the Trapper: "wonderful", "so amazing". He invites us both out to dinner once the interview is over. Huset is the obvious place to go, so we order a taxi. But it doesn't come, and it's a long wait with only three taxis in town. Eventually we agree to walk up, it will only take half an hour.

When we arrive at Huset the Anthropologist is huffing and puffing, "That was some walk!"

I don't bother translating this remark, which I assume is an aside for me. "Well, aren't you going to translate?" he nudges me.

What can I say? I turn to the trapper, "The anthropologist wants me to tell you that that was some walk."

The Trapper and I exchange a smile. He has just arrived in town after walking for three days from his cabin, crossing expanses of tundra, river deltas and a string of small mountains to get here.

At Huset our encounter turns into a game of musical chairs. I stay put but each time one of the men goes to the bathroom or to order food or drink at the counter the other takes the place where you can sit back to the wall.

At one point, when the Trapper is away from the table, the Anthropologist confesses to me, "Those photos, all that blood, how does he do it? It really made me feel sick..."

At the time I am disdainful of his hypocrisy. But more lenient in retrospect. The ability to single-handedly kill an animal and prepare its meat for consumption shocks the sensibilities of city-dwellers who are mostly far removed from the realities of slaughtering livestock or hunting. Our relationship with the animals that become our food is a vexed one.

I don't think he ever published his study. ▟

And so he is here, now; our paths have crossed again. Fact is stranger than fiction – if I wrote this into a novel, no one would believe me. Actually, this is a sort of novel, but that part is true – at least sort of. "Say hello from me," I say as the guests jump back into their Zodiac.

Saskia is preparing to sail out again that evening, and she has a new group of tourists due to arrive any moment now, so our visit has to be brief. Renata and I take our leave and Saskia takes us ashore. When and where will we meet again? In which continent or hemisphere? She revs the Zodiac and returns to the boat, looking back to wave one last time. We wave back and then turn to walk over towards the museum.

"Would you consider taking up your old job again?" asks Renata. I hesitate.

"Sometimes I get the feeling that life is a loop," I reply finally. "That there are points where it circles back and gives you the opportunity to pick things up where you left them. Even though years have gone by and you have had major life experiences in the interim. And if you do pick up at that point, it can seem like those major life experiences were mere parentheses. Do you know what I mean?"

"Maybe," she responds, "although I think I have experienced it the other way around. When I got my grant to study in China, I ended up in a village where I spent my whole day making earthenware and perfecting my knowledge of ceramics. I was happy and I think I could easily have stayed. But one day I woke up and realized I needed to get back to my real life. Looking back, it was just a dream, but when I was in it, it was very real. That was my life."

"Yes, sometimes it's hard to tell which level is the real level, and which level is the dream, don't you think? Kind of like that movie..." I continue.

"Yes, but I don't think you answered my question," she teases, and then exclaims, "Look up! There are two suns in the sky!"

"Sun dogs!" I have seen this only once before. Illusory suns caused by the refraction of light through ice crystals in the sky. They say they should appear on either side of the real sun, but today we see just one extra sun. We drink in this vision of twin orbs before going inside.

Books, paintings, artefacts. Black and white photos. Panels that quote old Arctic explorers. More books. The museum invites us to step back in time again, imagining this Arctic place in different periods, under different circumstances. Renata spends most of her time sitting on the sealskin-covered cushions on the floor, sketching the exhibits.

"I'm not sure about the whole sealskin thing," she mutters, "but the cushions are very comfortable." I understand her squeamishness. I was also brought up on images of white baby seals being beaten to death for their skins. But the situation here involves strict quotas, and Hiawatha would say, "This seal that I just killed was happy until the day it met me. Can you say the same about the cow or chicken that ended up on your plate?" He has a point. And when a seal is killed, every part of the animal is used, either for food or clothing.

"Renata, look at this!" I call. Not so much to show her the old dog sled in front of me, but because I recognize the text below it. It is one of the notices I translated for the museum many years before. Still there, like the recipes on the boat, despite the museum also having been transplanted from one site to another. So I have left my own small traces here, and not just my footprints in the earth. Some kind of personal punctuation mark – not a parenthesis in this case but maybe a comma or a semi-colon.

My gaze strays to a large illustrated book lying on a table, published recently by the looks of it, and I realize I know the author. The Anthropologist again.

Another sign? Or not? This one is not about trappers in any case. I flip through the pages of photos and move on to another book, "North of the desolate sea", written by Liv Balstad in 1958. She had come here as wife of the governor.

"There is no life here," writes Balstad. But I disagree. Life here is so manifold, from the multiple layers of flora and fauna and micro-organisms, to the curious goings-on of the people who came up to this northerly latitude over the centuries.

" * GOD HAS
ABANDONED THIS
PLACE, AND
HUMANS SHOULD
HAVE DONE SO
LONG AGO AS WELL."

NORD FOR DET ØDE HAV,
LIV BALSTAD
1956.

" (*) **Dette stedet**
er forlatt av Gud og
burde for lengst være
forlatt av mennesket også."

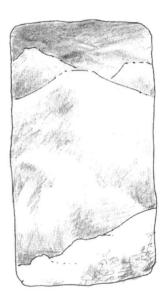

Crumbling marble (1997)

As we walk cautiously across the tundra, the burnt sienna of rusted metal contrasts with the eggshell blue sky. The weather seems to have softened the edges of the equipment and buildings that are gently fading into the landscape, although erosion is so slow in the Arctic that these remains are likely to live on for many hundreds of years yet.

Ny ("new") London is the site of a failed mining operation that caused a flurry of activity in the early 1900s before subsiding into oblivion. Abandoned buildings, a metal locomotive and the tracks it used to run on, a wooden wheelbarrow. All bear witness to a few people's dreams and the power of persuasion of Ernest Mansfield, a charismatic explorer and business developer - as well as journalist and poet - who convinced people to contribute to what became the biggest bubble of the day on the London stock market, his marble mining venture. The marble of Blomstrandhalvøya was said to rival that of Carrera in Italy, from which Michelangelo's finest works are sculpted.

Except that the Svalbard marble crumbled when it was shipped to warmer climes. Worthless.

Mansfield was dismissed from the leadership of the Northern Exploration Company. And Ny London was left to decay.

We step carefully around the remains of this brief enterprise, and head back to the boat. ▰

"We're closing now." We are the last visitors in the museum and they are throwing us out. We collect our bicycles and make our way back up to Nybyen.

By this time Renata, Jon and I have become a fixed friendship group, and we meet up every day. I wonder if the bonds of these few days spent together are stronger than those that tie me to my semi-estranged companions of previous years. Or just more immediate. Facilitated by the limbo that we share, the limbo of travellers, of people passing through.

Tonight we're tired of cooking in the hostel kitchen, and decide to go back down to Kroa, this time for dinner.

Together with café Busen, Kroa used to be one of the bases of my social triangle (Huset was the apex). Busen no longer exists – it has metamorphosed into a Thai restaurant – but Kroa is much the same. Kroa was where I both met and missed people, it had its own special vibe.

Time warp (1995)

I have arranged to meet up at Kroa with the German and some visitors he has in town. I had a nap in the afternoon and lost track of the hour so it is quite late by the time I start walking down. I am almost there when a taxi comes by. It stops for me and the passenger says, "Hop in, I'll give you a lift." "But I'm only going down there," I protest, pointing to Kroa a few hundred metres down the road.

"It doesn't matter, we're polite here in Svalbard," he replies. I am a bit bewildered but this is a trust-based community and I climb in. But as we drive up we see it is already closed. "Oh. Don't worry. I'll give you a ride back to your place," says the man. "But that's back in Nybyen!" I exclaim. He steps out and pays the taxi driver to drive me back up. For some reason my watch has been running an hour slow, and the whole sequence is becoming a surrealist tableau as one incomprehension melts into the next.

I am home and about to go to bed when one of my neighbours bursts in. He is a plumber who works in the mines. We run into each other every day and exchange polite

hellos. But tonight he is dishevelled and clutching a
bottle of vodka. "Come and join us," he shouts. "There's
a party on in the block next door." I hesitate, but I
can't resist this invitation to what will be my first
true Longyearbyen party.

Everyone is somewhere fairly advanced on a contin-
uum of drunkenness and I feel out of sync. But someone
puts on a Dylan album and the words and heartbeat rhythm
compensate for my sobriety ...*and your pleasure knows
no limits, your voice is like a meadowlark... but your
heart is like an ocean, mysterious and dark...* Petter is
there and we find ourselves dancing together, and I can
feel we are perfectly harmonized, bodies close, moving to the poetry. But he pulls away before the end of
the song. "Do you know you have a pencil in your shirt
pocket?" he asks. I always have a pencil and at least
one folded sheet of paper in a pocket, in case I need to
record a fleeting thought. I remove it, but the moment
has passed.

And then we are sitting on the floor, the alcohol
is flowing freely but the flow of everything else has
thickened, the air is like liquid glass. The party or-
ganizers have made an effort to darken the apartment to
create a night-time atmosphere, but the covering has
fallen from one of the windows. In the bright sunlight
pouring in I see a young woman slowly take the hand of
the young man in front of her. They look into each other's eyes, but somehow the air is too viscous for them to
move beyond that. Petter is watching, incredulous, and
I realize that she is the girlfriend of his friend the
Journalist, who is not there to witness this betrayal
in slow motion. Although fidelity is not one of Petter's

core values I can read on his face that he thinks he should do something. He speaks, but it doesn't seem like there is any point intervening in anything, and anyway it would have been too slow, like in those dreams where you are on the railway tracks and the train is coming but your body is too heavy to stand. Or you know you can fly, but when danger approaches your body turns to lead and you can no longer lift off, flapping your arms helplessly.

The scene becomes unbearable and I stand and find my way outside to get some air. The cold brings me back up to normal speed and I decide to go home.

I check my watch before going to bed and fall into a deep sleep. Sleep and wake and look at the time. 9 a.m.? I am so tired, but surely I've had enough sleep, even though I went to bed at 2? Yet I can hardly keep my eyes open, and am shivering with cold. I don't feel hungry at all, but I have a bite to eat, all rugged up in bed, just to get the internal motor going.

I keep looking at my watch - is it really 9 a.m. already? Everything seems different. I can't see the sun in its usual place, but maybe because the clouds have rolled in and the sky is grey and overcast? No noise to be heard in the house either, and no builders working over the road. I am very confused.

Am I in a time warp? I check my watch one more time. It reads 3.30 a.m. - I had been looking at it upside down. I fall back into bed and wake in the morning with the feeling that everything is right with the world again. I call the German to explain what happened and the episode consolidates my reputation as a Bridget Jones kind of girl. Not that anyone used the term "Bridget Jones" yet. ▨

I still associate Kroa specifically with the German. It's where we used to go that first year to pick up a thick-crust cheesy pizza after a long day out walking or filming. I suddenly miss him – his wry sense of humour and the outsider's perspective he had on this place. What would he say now about the changes rippling through this town?

We find a free table and place our orders. Jon buys a first round of beers. We have been drinking only Arctic Beer for the past few days in honour of the Kid.

"I'm going to miss you guys when you leave tomorrow," sighs Jon.

We are going to miss him too. "Jon – please send us photos!"

"Of course – and I want to see your book, or play, or whatever it is."

"I'm nearly done with the play part," I say, "although I sent a draft to my friend Henri the theatre critic and he intimated that it was hard to follow. I think he means that it needs a complete rewrite. Anyway, let me know what you think."

Renata offers to get the next round of beers. She is a bit slow and our meals have arrived by the time she gets back. The food extinguishes conversation for a while so it takes me a while to realize that Renata is staring into space. "Are you okay?" I ask.

"Er, yes, everything's fine," she replies, "I was just lost in thought." She doesn't seem to want to share where her mind went.

ARCTIC BEER.
WE RAISE A TOAST
TO THE KID.

Day 7
Pathways

It is our last day. Winding down with gentle exploration. Renata and I ride our bicycles inland, towards the end of the road in Adventdalen. There is hardly any traffic, there are no tourist destinations down this way, although there are some research stations and private cabins owned by Longyearbyen residents.

We stop near the end of the road and observe the reindeer grazing peacefully, packing in the summer calories before winter hits. We sit down for our own snack of nuts and chocolate before turning back towards town.

I am riding a few metres ahead when I hear a cry behind me, "Wait!"

Renata's bicycle is playing up again. This time the pedal is not only getting stuck but actually falls off. We resign ourselves to walking back. It's a bit of a way, but we don't have any choice. At least we have a gun now and don't have to worry about it getting dark. And it's an opportunity to talk a bit more instead of shouting into the wind on our bicycles.

"So will you tell me what happened yesterday at Kroa?" I ask. "You didn't seem your usual self at dinner."

"Yeah, I didn't feel like telling you at the time, but I had a very intense encounter."

Renata hesitates and then continues, "You and Jon were talking and I was standing at the bar, doodling in my notebook while I was waiting for our beers when I heard a whisper from behind a curtain of silky blond hair, 'Who draws so well?'

"I could smell her scent near my cheek and mumbled awkwardly in response, 'It must be this pen…' She came so close I could even smell the beer on her breath but I didn't know what to do. I wasn't expecting a local beauty to show interest in a middle-aged woman like me. I offered to buy Janike a coffee the other day and she wasn't interested at all.

"We exchanged a few words in a mix of languages. She started telling me about her teacher's job, but then stopped abruptly and I could see a man over at one of the tables gesturing to her. She leaned close to my ear and whispered, 'You and I have to talk. I'll be back in a few minutes. Wait here for me.' I didn't believe her. I came to sit with you, but when I glanced back I saw that she was at the bar again, looking for me. I was paralysed. And when I looked around again, she was gone. That's why I had that vacant expression on my face when you asked me what was wrong.

"Strangely enough, I had a dream about her this morning. The two of us were in bed but it was very chaste, and we were talking about birds and the Arctic Ocean. I knew that our relationship was destined to fail and I started writing a short story about how couples fall apart when they overcome the language barrier. But the Arctic waves were splashing over the letters on the page and everything started to disintegrate, the characters floating away like black spots into the froth of the sea. Sea that was bubbling and whispering, close to my cheek – like the froth on a beer in a Longyearbyen bar…"

"Oh Renata," I exclaim, "I had no idea!" Renata is typically so reserved that she has caught me by surprise with this story of seduction. "I was surprised too," she grins.

"Including about Janike," I add. "How did you manage to flirt with the receptionist without me noticing?"

Just then a pick-up truck appears out of nowhere and the driver invites us to stack our bicycles in the back and pile in. Which we do, sitting three in a row with a retired miner we later learn is known as the Professor. He insists on taking us to his workshop, where he repairs the bicycle, all the time telling us about his profound love of the Arctic. He can't bring himself to move back to the continent.

I tell him I spent time in Svalbard many years ago, "But so much has changed! These new neighbourhoods here. And even the glaciers, I can hardly recognize them, they've retreated so much."

"Yes, it's true, things change. Although you can't be 100 percent sure about why the glaciers have retreated. There can be many contributing factors, soot from ship traffic for example, which settles on the snow and ice and causes it to melt." So if it's not climate change, it's pollution. I wonder which is worse.

He hands over Renata's bicycle, which he has managed to tweak so that the pedal works again. Renata has of course been sketching in the meantime, and gives him the rough portrait she has just done. She has captured perfectly his face and eyes, which have a Santa-like kindliness without the banal naivety – in fact he looks a bit like my Uncle Otto, who has his own Christmas-tree stand near Frogner park in Oslo each year. They embrace and exchange emails. I feel like the third wheel, but then we all say goodbye and Renata and I ride back to the guesthouse to pack and check out and get ready for our last dinner.

THE PROFESSOR

This year we saw 1500 reindeer.
A record! Maybe it's climate
change, less cold weather and
more to eat.

THE OLD-TIMER PICKED US UP WHEN MY BICYCLE
PEDAL BROKE. HE EVEN TOOK US TO HIS
WORKSHOP TO FIX IT.

Back to the future (1994)

Only two weeks left. Another night of disturbed sleep despite the fact that I have had such a full day. I am beginning to feel hemmed in – I need time away from the town, the closed-in feeling of Longyearbyen valley. I never would have imagined that I could feel this way in this remotest of all towns.

Adventdalen is long and wide. It is not hard terrain to walk in, but rather soft and spongy and green. The reindeer love it. The only tricky part about these big wide valleys is the rivers. Where is it best to cross? This has been part of my local life lessons. Upstream they are narrower but often too deep to cross if there are not conveniently located stones and boulders to provide jumping points. Too far down, they pan out, but this can mean a lot of extra walking and sometimes they still run too high. Rivers swell and subside, depending on temperature, cloud cover and time of day, the glacier melt changing with the angle of the sun.

It is always good to have some waders for these big valley rivers. As long as you have at least two pairs someone can carry the other ones back for the others.

But I am alone and without waders today. And in any case I am not going to cross the main river.

I leave my bicycle by the road at the opening to the first side valley, Endalen, the poetically named Valley One, situated just before Todalen (you can guess what that means). And off I go through the stones and water and marsh and springy cushions of earth and vegetation, feeling like some kind of anachronistic duck shooter with the rifle slung over my shoulder. I am still not quite used to this.

Idiosyncratic reindeer, noses in the air, prance along. Sometimes they watch me, back off when I move towards them, but start following me as soon as I have turned away.

Endalen is V-shaped like Longyear valley, with the difference that nobody lives here, at least not permanently. There are a few cabins sprinkled near the opening of the valley, where some people like to spend their spare time, away from the madding crowd.

I pick my way slowly up the side and along towards the glacier behind. I am not so familiar with its sides and paths, the best way to circumnavigate the moraine. My curiosity is rewarded by the unexpected waterfall that cuts through the rock at the back of the valley, the blue and white and rocky view that stretches out behind me once I rise above the valley floor. I prefer heights to valleys. Changes. The glacier. The water. The fossils. The sun suddenly bright. I find a place to sit and break open a Kvikk Lunsj chocolate bar. And then I lie back for a moment, staring up at the sky.

But I have work awaiting me in Longyearbyen - it is time to return.

After walking back down Endalen, I collect my bicycle and head along the broad floor of the main valley towards Longyearbyen. It could be a boring ride – the road is fairly straight. But I settle into a sort of timelessness, as the absent-minded sun moves slowly around behind the layer of cloud as though it will always be the same day.

The usual landmarks punctuate the route back: the mire that often hosts a solitary red-throated diver sitting serenely on a small clod in the middle of the water, the reservoir where the light changes as I cycle past. There is a break in the clouds above Longyearbyen. The town is glowing, luminous curtains of rain shifting between the valleys. Water and light.

In the distance I see a small cloud of dust approaching, signalling a vehicle. The four-wheel drive pulls up beside me. "Hey Marianne – I see you've been out for a walk? I have a fax for you," – and Ibsen stretches out his arm with a rolled-up fax, emanating that then familiar thermal paper smell, so incongruous on this Arctic road.

He has switched off the engine. Silence and emptiness stretch out in all directions. The town is just a suggestion in the distance. It occurs to me that Ibsen has appeared from some other time to hand me this anachronistic document, and that perhaps I am a character in a film like *Back to the Future*. Although the fax is just a note from the Anthropologist. He wants me to call to discuss some new ideas.

I thank Ibsen and get back on my bicycle, and he continues on his way, wherever that was. It is late when I get back to town, but late doesn't really have much meaning here. ▨

To mark our departure, Hiawatha has invited us to join him for dinner. He lives near the airport, so we pack our bags early and say goodbye to Jon, Psy-Girl and Country Counter at the guest house. "I really feel like we are old friends," says Jon as we all hug, "even though we've only known each other for a week."

The others will all be staying a few more days. We deliver our gun and bicycles back to Tom the Bike, who offers to drop us off at Hiawatha's place. "But before I do, I'd like to show you something," he says. We drive down to Block 1 and he unlocks the door. "Recognize this?" he asks. We are in the office I used to work in. It looks different now, but I see that he is pointing to a rock by the door. It dawns on me that it is the petrified wood that the Geologist and I rolled down the hill from the moraine a couple of decades before, and that I left in the custody of Tall Viking. "You may not realize it, but you are known for this lump of rock," he winks. "My brother still tells the tale."

We jump back in the van and he runs us down to the big green house by the shore. We take the liberty of giving him a hug too as we say goodbye. I guess the occasional squeeze is okay. "And don't forget to say hello to your brother," I call as he climbs back into his van.

The door to the house is open and we walk straight in. We find Hiawatha scraping a pipe to remove some dried glue, and it sounds to me like a güiro, a Peruvian percussion instrument made from a gourd cut with parallel notches that you scratch with a stick. I mention this and it inspires him to put some songs of El Pajaro Campana on his old cassette player. For some reason Hiawatha has a collection of Latin American folk music, which provides the sound track for that last evening up north.

He invites us to sit down, uncorks one of the bottles of Chilean white wine that we have bought from the restricted wine section of the store, and starts preparing the Arctic char that he has fished himself. "It's such a hassle with the Sysselmann these days, you have to write down and declare everything you catch…" He is referring to the new

TIME TO PACK UP.
I WONDER IF MARIANNE
WILL ACTUALLY EVER
WRITE THIS BOOK.

regulations brought in by the governor, it's a recurrent theme and we fight about it every time. "Of course there have to be rules and quotas," I counter. I guess the secret is the balance, never easy to find.

His cabin is perfectly placed to see the sunset. We won't be here to see it, we will be leaving Longyearbyen before it starts touching the horizon, but it is close enough now to give us that warm golden sunset glow. The setting sun always a sign that it's time to go south again.

The bay of July (1996)

The water is so still that a film of ice has formed on the surface. An idea. A suggestion of crystals. We can see it forming before our eyes. Slightly misting up the otherwise perfect mirror. The boat cuts through it. Ever so gently.

And the landscape is infinitely gentle with us. The boat is suspended between water and mountains and sky above and below.

I decide to sleep outside, on deck. Today, tonight, the sun dips to its lowest point yet.

I had forgotten the existence of the colour pink in the sky, but now a rose-coloured blush fills the horizon and its reflection in the shimmer of ice and reminds me that time exists. It is not an unwelcome return. My nose is cold but otherwise I am snug and warm in my sleeping bag and this first homage to evening sings my spirit to sleep.

Skipper Sr has always called this place the bay of Julie. But earlier today he pointed at the map and asked me why there is always a number 14 in front of the name. I laugh and tell him he's not a true Frenchman. It's the 14th of July, Bastille Day. Not a woman's name at all. ▨

We drink wine while Hiawatha shows us his gun collection. I am a bit blasé about the whole thing, I guess I'm pretty sure he has spent enough time with guns to avoid unintentional mishap. Renata however is alarmed. "Why doesn't he just put that pistol away?" she turns to me at one point. We have all had too much to drink.

He has cooked us a succulent fish meal, and we reflect on life and language – we are navigating the conversation across three or four languages, but it works. Hiawatha is no longer holding back on the critiques, "Your Norwegian has really deteriorated, you know. I hope you're no longer doing translations." But I take it with a grain of salt.

The conversation turns to creativity and invention – Hiawatha designed and built an impressive number of things during the solitary hours in his trapper's cabin, including a whole electrical system and a machine for cleaning the down that he collects from the eider ducks.

"So did you make any progress on your book?" he asks. "I have the first draft of a short play," I reply. "But I'm not sure if it works."

"It doesn't really end on an optimistic note," remarks Renata. Which suits her, she thinks we need to shake people up.

"But didn't they actually succeed in creating a utopia in the original by Aristophanes?" asks Hiawatha.

"Well, that's what many critics say," I reply, "but I don't buy it. I don't think Aristophanes would have promoted greed and colonization as a pathway to utopia, would he?"

Tom the Bike has printed out the typescript for me at the guest house, and I hand a copy to Hiawatha for him to read after we have left.

And then we realize it is time to get to the airport for our flight back to Oslo. After two bottles of wine as well as some aquavit, no one is in a fit state to drive, so we decide to walk. Hiawatha assures us that we can take a shortcut across the tundra to the airport, so we heave our bags up onto our shoulders and make our way in that direction.

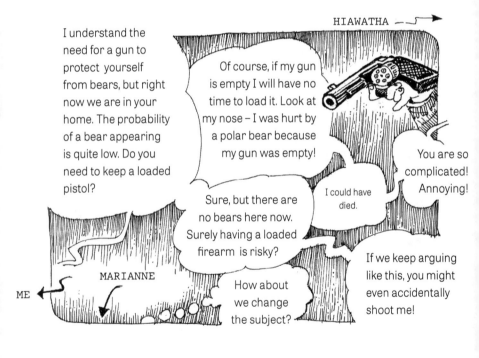

We hug. And then speak a bit more. And then one last hug. "See you soon, I hope." Renata echoes my words, although she knows she is probably less likely to return than I am.

"Yeah, maybe," replies Hiawatha. He promises to keep an eye out for bears on our behalf as we walk over to the airport – and by this point we know that he has more than enough guns at the ready. But it is the birds that attack. We tread as respectfully as possible but first the terns and then the Arctic skua are wheeling and diving angrily and have no patience for our intrusion onto their territory. These birds are not willing to cede their sovereignty just yet.

I'm pretty sure I can see someone laughing back at the house, and I briefly wonder whether this is a set-up.

We build in a detour and manage to avoid the menacing birds. When we reach the asphalt of the terminal it occurs to us that it is a strange and incongruous site. The light inside seems wrong, no longer thick and golden but weak and white. I scan the clusters of people, unconsciously looking out for the German, or maybe even Petter. But there is no one I recognize. The flight is due to leave at 4 a.m., so we sit half-asleep against a wall until it is time to board our flight.

ARCTIC TERN

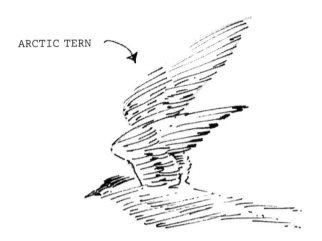

THE BIRDS OF SVALBARD
CERTAINLY DEFEND THEIR
TERRITORY. THE TERNS ARE
ESPECIALLY AGGRESSIVE.

THIS ONE SPOTTED ME
AND DIVED DOWN TO
SCARE ME AWAY.

August farewell (1997)

Last day in Longyearbyen. For now at least. Curtains of fog are hanging from the crumbling rods protruding from the plateau, which I observe through the window of Busen café. The girl serving lunch has an accent from the south of Norway that can be heard above the murmur of conversation at the different tables.

The old timers say it is not like it used to be. But Busen is still, then, the place of the counter lunch and the serendipitous encounter. Serene afternoons of coffee spills, refills and reasonable bills.

I look through the window and write sporadically. Chat to people who sit down with me for a while, and then leave as others take their place. The Trapper comes in, not Hiawatha but the other one I met while translating for the Anthropologist. He is accompanied by Petter. I didn't know they knew each other, although I guess pretty much everyone knows everyone else here. Petter goes over to the bar to order while the Trapper stops to talk to me briefly. I admire his necklace of seal claws, which he gives to me as a farewell present and then walks over to where Petter is and they sit and drink coffee and chat for a while. I don't know what happened to that necklace, I no longer have it. I think it must have joined the realm of lost things at some point over the years, together with the musk ox pelt that Uncle Otto gave me.

And then the Trapper takes his leave and Petter comes over and takes a seat opposite me. We haven't been talking much, but he knows I am leaving today so he stays for a while. We speak about peace of mind, the peace of mind that solitude brings here, when out, alone, just looking at the landscape. The importance of travelling towards things, rather than away – this is the impetus of life, not looking back, nostalgically, as I am perhaps – uncharacteristically – doing now. When he hugs me goodbye, his nutmeg scent lingers thickly in a way that seems at odds with his lean frame and translucent skin.

Perhaps Longyearbyen has made me oversensitive to smell. When I arrive in Tromsø it is like returning to the tropics. The sky Kandinsky blue, it feels impossible to drink in all the heady fragrances of summer, after that thin almost imperceptible coal odour of Longyearbyen, only rarely punctuated by something stronger.

As I write my life I am rewriting it, but then, my mind did that already. Consciousness in its selective and subjective interpretation changes all these memories each time it recalls them. But maybe smell brings back the most accurate of memories? That rush of recollection that suddenly comes to you with the whiff of a forgotten smell. The least virtual of the virtual reality of consciousness? Where actual molecules from outside enter you and lock in with your mind.

My dear friend the German drives me to the airport and waves goodbye as I board the plane. ▨

The boarding sign has come up on the display. It's time to leave. As we all exit the gate and passengers start to mill across the tarmac towards the plane I pause for a moment. The air is dry. My cheeks are aflame and my lips feel as though they have been kissed by the wind all night, or rather day that is not night. A dust cloud from a passing car obscures temporarily the clarity of the air. By the time the powder blue sky reasserts itself, I am already in the plane.

Day 0
Portals

Only Renata seems to understand why there is another Day 0. That we have completed a loop.

I am walking along a path in shadow, in a park perhaps or a forest or even a city, or maybe all of those at once. I come to a church or a cave and go inside. I pass through a space of darkness and come out the other side into a sort of garden, a cloister with paths that lead into the distance. There are quite a few people around, like tourists in the south of France, and the whole area is bathed in autumn light. I look up at the sky and see almost tangible sunbeams coming through the clouds. I realize suddenly that the time has changed. It is not the same time here in the garden as it was on the other side of the church-cave. The sun is not in the same place. I am afraid, afraid that I will not be able to get back to the other side, and at the same time full of wonder.

I do go back through to the other side however and see that Saskia is there. I tell her about the beautiful place and bring her through and show her. Being a sailor and navigator she measures the angle of the sun's rays and concludes that we are in a different universe. We both become afraid and don't want to stay here too long even though it is so awe-inspiring. As we are walking back through the church-cave I run into the Kid and marvel at this coincidence. I try to fathom the different universes and have a vision of the continent of Europe, like a map, being twisted, almost wrung, and it seems to me it is a heart being wrung of its love.

I wake up and lie in bed for a while, trying to get my bearings. Then I tiptoe out through the living room towards the bathroom, trying not to disturb Renata, but I see she is awake too and tell her my dream.

We are back in Oslo, staying at Gøril's place. I've only mentioned her once before and we haven't ever met. We won't meet her now either because she is away somewhere travelling. It is Eli again, Eli from the beginning of this story, another destiny interchange, linking people together through her web of friendships. There are comfortable chairs, good books and interesting paintings at Gøril's. She already feels like a friend. And her home feels like home for the brief time we are there.

We meet up with Eli and Liv – you remember her, right, the artist who works at the Opera – for breakfast at a nearby bakery as planned. The bread is not as good as the loaves that Liv bakes, with crushed cardamom seeds that bring unexpected bursts of flavour. But the sticky buns sprinkled with coconut flakes taste of my childhood and are one of my Oslo rituals.

They are plying us with questions about our trip when Eli stands, calling out, "Over here!" It is the Kid. I haven't seen him in years, we lost touch after he moved from Paris to the Middle East. I had heard he was back in Oslo but hadn't managed to find him. But I'm not surprised that Eli did. The story of the Kid and our reunion is too long and convoluted to tell here. I hope he will tell it himself one day.

For now let's just say that everything is connected.

Renata spends the day at the Edvard Munch museum while I carry out some errands. I pick her up there and we jump on a tram to Uncle Bjørn's who is expecting us for dinner. "I was afraid you wouldn't find me," Renata tells me afterwards. "We never did agree on an exact time or place to meet up."

Uncle Otto and my cousins are there too. Uncle Bjørn is a passionate horticulturalist and chef and he has prepared a delicate cucumber salad with petals from the violets in his garden. We speak about Svalbard and Greenland and art and my cousins' poodles, and the child that my youngest cousin would like to have. I am missing my own

WE DIDN'T AGREE ON A MEETING
TIME BUT MARIANNE TURNED UP
JUST AS I WAS COMING OUT.

daughters. It is time to go home, to return to that part of myself. This is a good half-way house, among my Norwegian family, where I can safely shed one skin and begin to reassume the other.

Renata gives my two uncles the line drawings she has done that day, variations on the theme of Munch's *The Scream*. Renata's renditions are a little warmer, a little less anguished, than the original. And then my older cousin drops us back to Gøril's. It is still relatively early in the evening, around 9 p.m.

"I'm sure you were secretly hoping you would run into Petter on this trip?" asks Renata. "But why don't you just call? I bet he would be happy to hear from you, even if it has been a long time. He is an important part of this story – this is your chance to close the loop. Look him up."

Is it really as simple as that? I step outside the frame for a moment and remind myself that he is not real, but rather woven from different threads, including something of myself, a self that I buried when I stopped heading north each summer.

It's okay, I say. I think I already found what I was looking for.

Renata has an early flight and we wake at 3 a.m. to make sure we get to the station in time for her to catch the airport bus. Gøril's place is within walking distance and we make our way through the empty city towards the terminal.

When we arrive we are not quite sure of the way in. The usual entrance is closed and we circle around in the dark trying to find an opening. On the carpark side we see some young people pulling their suitcases through a small door. As the last person exits, I run over, grab it before it can slam shut and we enter. But we are not going into the fiction, we are leaving it behind. Stepping back outside.

I WOULD HAVE LIKED TO HAVE
SPOKEN MORE WITH OTTO BUT HE
COULDN'T HEAR VERY WELL.

MARIANNE'S
UNCLE OTTO

HER COUSIN ANNE

HER
COUSIN'S
POODLE

This is my
boyfriend,
Jan-Erik.

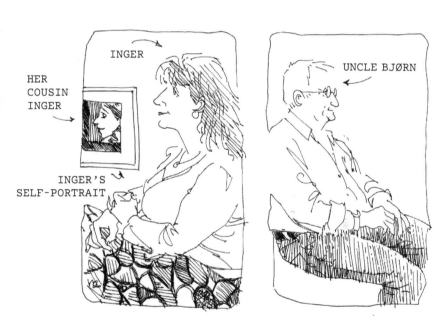

INGER

HER
COUSIN
INGER

INGER'S
SELF-PORTRAIT

UNCLE BJØRN

MARIANNE'S UNCLE PREPARED A SALAD
WITH PETALS FROM THE GARDEN.

Afterword

This place is not my place. And especially at this time. The place I am writing about is a fiction, or some kind of dream, or maybe it is just the intersection between a real place and me. This intersection is the only legitimate claim I have to any kind of voice.

The people I write about, and even those I am writing to, are different degrees of real. Vikings, trappers, sailors, dead poets and their translated daughters... Maybe you recognize some of them, or even yourself. Thank you for letting me play with the places and times and ways in which we crossed paths. Friendship is the truest form of love, the least possessive. No friend or hometown ever forced me to stay, or ever said I could never come back. I am lucky. Some of my friends' homes or cities have become war zones or have been ravaged by environmental disasters, no return possible.

Nevertheless, if you stay away too long things shift, the light changes, the community evolves, the land itself changes. Not just war, or development, but nature itself can slowly sweep away the foundations of a place where you lived. Nature and the effects of relentless human activity, even in locations far removed. And people come and go. In this Arctic town, people are not born and are not even supposed to die. They wash through faster than in many other places, as their lives move on and take them elsewhere.

But I have found you at the crossroads. I hope I will find you again.

Rewind

what remains?
the days when the misty eyelid opened
translucent sky replacing greys
or the firns losing face
under the gaze of the incessant daylight

a glass breaks, god rays
infiltrate the low cloud
casting our leaden shadows in long lines
against the rows of houses,
subverting the colour code

the late August sun is on amber
teasing the horizon
former lives rush up like infidels
inviting transgression

a rewriting of the intervals
a stitching back up of the scenes
nothing is what it seems

The Birds

Based on the play by Aristophanes (414 B.C.)

Characters

PAULSEN	Scandinavian entrepreneur
JUELSEN	Scandinavian entrepreneur, friend and associate of Juelsen
SANDPIPER	Footbird to the Sysselmann
SNOW PTARMIGAN	Sysselmann (governor)
CHORUS OF BIRDS	
TERN	Leader of the Birds
GREY GOOSE	Messenger 1
PINK-FOOTED GOOSE	Messenger 2
BARNACLE GOOSE	Messenger 3
INSPECTOR	
LAWYER	
INFORMER	
QUEEN AMAZOOM	Sky-high tech representative
WACKY PETE	Member of sky-high tech delegation
NESPECTACLE	Member of sky-high tech delegation
RENTAROOM	Member of sky-high tech delegation
TRIBALLIAN	Barbarian god

Scene 1

Juelsen and Paulsen, two dissatisfied entrepreneurs
from southern Scandinavia who were sailing north to
earn some easy money and prepare for their retirement,
are lost at sea.

JUELSEN
 Is it this way?

PAULSEN
 Or that way?

JUELSEN
 We're lost.

PAULSEN
 You don't say!

JUELSEN
 And there's no turning back.
 You've got a real knack for leading
 us up the creek.
 Was that heatwave so bad
 that we had to pack in our jobs for a
 few bytes of bitcoin?

PAULSEN
 "Head north," the agent said,
 "it's really cool.
 You won't be disappointed,
 you'd be a fool
 to say no." He gave his word.

JUELSEN
 Yeah, I guess we bought his plan,
 thought we'd find the promised land,
 "To get there, just point your
 compass and look for the birds…"

PAULSEN
I would have downloaded a maps app if
we could connect to a network.
Too bad Waze is out of range…

JUELSEN
We've been going round in circles for
days.

PAULSEN
How can you tell? The sun never sets.

JUELSEN
Well, you can't even tell east from
west.

PAULSEN
Maybe, but by the looks of it there's
something ahead.
I've got a signal, hang on, Maps says
this way.

JUELSEN
Huh, that app's like the oracle,
says whatever you want it to say.
I'd look out for a gull,
a more reliable sign of land I say.

PAULSEN (to audience)
We know, it seems strange
that we, legit citizens of a sought-
after place, decide to emigrate,
while others fake papers and squeeze
their lives into a suitcase
just to get into our space.
But you see, it's that lately it's
been getting so warm
and I saw this link on my feed –
itgothot dot com:

"Sick of sweating through June, July
and August?
Want to get out of town or buy to
invest?
There's opportunities up north,
don't leave it too late.
No incremental taxes,
just a flat rate,
and by modern standards
the weather is great
and getting more attractive year
after year.
You too can be pioneers of the latest
frontier.
Just sign on the dotted line… Here!
Not to mention all the geological
treasures.
There's plenty of potential for new
economic ventures.
Greenland is Greenlandic, it's hard
to tap into its ores.
But this archipelago is up for grabs,
its resources could be all yours…"

To get back to us, we'd like a nice
spot to retire
and in a plus three scenario even
Oslo's a bit dire
and we could do with a rainy day fund
while we're here.
So if we can sell the idea –
well, we're sure there'll be buyers.

Scene 2

In which Paulsen and Juelsen reach the realm of the
birds and prepare to present their plan.

(the two companions reach land and pull their boat up
on the sand, shortly after which a bird appears from
nowhere)

>SANDPIPER (footbird)
>Who's this? Who seeks out the
>Sysselmann?

>PAULSEN
>Sysselmann? What's a Sysselmann?
>We're humans from a distant land.
>Listen up, man, we're here to pitch a
>new plan!

>SANDPIPER
>First, don't call me "man". I'm a
>bird, is that clear?
>As for the Sysselmann - he's the
>guv'nor, the boss around here.
>But you should have emailed us first,
>you can't just appear.

>JUELSEN
>But we signed up, itgothot dot com
>said we were on the list.

>SANDPIPER
>Hmm, are you lawyers, taxmen, or
>scientists?

>PAULSEN
>We're entrepreneurs and we want to
>fly with the birds.
>We hear it's de rigueur for self-
>respecting adventurers.
>And we're no amateurs, rest assured…

SANDPIPER
  That's absurd...
  (interrupted by arrival of the Snow
  Ptarmigan)

SNOW PTARMIGAN (SYSSELMANN)
  Good day, I'm here, what do you have
  to say?

JUELSEN
  Hello, dear ptarmigan, nice to meet
  you, enchanté!
  (bursting into song)
  Well, you see, we'd like to live in
  this land up above
  where, we hear, birds like to breed
  and share the love.
  But not only is this already a
  prime location,
  we reckon we can help you grow your
  station...

PAULSEN
  ...into a self-sufficient independent
  nation.

SNOW PTARMIGAN
  Really, and how d'you think you'd go
  about it?

PAULSEN
  Well, first, with a wall to keep
  interlopers out. It's
  true all big leaders are building
  walls these days.
  It makes places great and losers
  stay away.
  At these latitudes, anywhere north

of 70 degrees
is prime real estate for climate
expats and retirees
who are planning for the next 10
years or so.
In another 20 I'm sure we can even
make crops grow
or vines, if you want to try
your hand at wine.
Mining's promising, and the sailing
routes are still free:
Take over the north passages and
you'll be reeling in the booty.

SNOW PTARMIGAN
Hmm, we'll have to run this by the
local council.
I'm sold, but I think they may be
doubtful.

JUELSEN
Who'll put it to them?

SNOW PTARMIGAN
Why you of course.
They're not wild fowl,
I've taught them the arts of
discourse.
I'll call them now,
then the stage is yours.

Scene 3

Where the birds convene to listen to the development
proposal and Paulsen and Juelsen convince them to
accept.

SNOW PTARMIGAN
Dear birds, let's give a warm
greeting
to these gentlemen who have come all
this way for a meeting.
They'd like to share some ideas for
development.
They're distinguished entrepreneurs,
their goals are benevolent.

JUELSEN
Never even seen half these breeds of
bird before.

PAULSEN
A beaut' collection, but if they
attack I reckon we're done for.

SNOW PTARMIGAN
Come along dear birds and join the
caucus.
The orchestra is lovely, but don't be
too raucous.
Again, let's greet these men warmly
so we can get on and start the
meeting formally.

TERN (chorus leader)
You've betrayed us, you fool!
Letting people in, that's breaking
the rules.
Let me pull in my death squads and
we'll peck out their eyeballs.

No exceptions allowed to the terms
and conditions.
Stand proud, we terns will grant no
admission.
Brother skuas, stand steady now,
beaks at the ready
to skewer these intruders with their
dangerous ambitions.

JUELSEN
Help!

PAULSEN
How do we defend ourselves
now from these avian demons escaped
from hell?

SNOW PTARMIGAN
Calm down you skuas, kittiwakes and
terns.
Keep still and tune in to our
visitors' words.
You may consider that you've nothing
to learn
from your natural enemies,
but now it's their turn
to speak and to show they appreciate
your concerns.

TERN
Why are they intruding in our polar
sanctuary?

SNOW PTARMIGAN
Lend them an ear.
Paulson has an idea
that he's anxious to share,
thinks it'll be good for society.

TERN
　We'll hear him out, but he'd better
　be quick.

PAULSEN
　You birds here are big
　and your natural parks are valuable
　digs.
　You could make lots of money keeping
　people cool.
　They're already heading north, so if
　you assert your rule
　you can develop this land with houses
　and pools,
　a golf course, even a mall - but
　first you need a wall.
　Anyone - giants, humans and all -
　going in or out will have to pay a
　toll.

TERN
　But governments will say we're in
　violation
　of multilateral rules and
　regulations.
　They'll say we're using
　intimidation.

PAULSEN
　Nah, you'll see, it's the money that
　counts.
　They'll be bowing down to you without
　any doubt.
　Our Sysselmann here can make you
　senior civil servants
　so you'll be observing the protocol,
　no need to be nervous.

Or - even better - create a company.
Taxes are low.

TERN
But men don't just want comfort,
they also want dough.

PAULSEN
Then I suggest a polar pyramid
scheme:
Make them real estate agents and
boost your revenue stream.

TERN
Hmm, that seems pretty nifty.
Let me know if I got it:
We create lots, rent out plots,
make a lot of money off of it
and divvy up the profit?

PAULSEN
That's right, and you'll be able to
live better too
if you're the ones telling the
governments what to do.

JUELSEN
We've got to start with a publicity
campaign.

PAULSEN
First of all, let's give this place a
name!

JUELSEN
Let's call it the "Cold Coast",
sounds exclusive.

PAULSEN
Yeah, sounds cool.

TERN
It'll do.

SNOW PTARMIGAN
The evidence is conclusive.

JUELSEN
I'll spread it across the
twittersphere.

PAULSEN
Leave that to the birds, you start
building the wall over here.

JUELSEN
Do we need to report back to itgothot
dot com?

PAULSEN
Nah, it's time for our own spot in
the midnight sun.

Scene 4

Where Paulsen and Juelsen begin construction of a wall
while fending off bureaucrats and rival profiteers.

PAULSEN
Hey, get on with the building!

JUELSEN
No, I'm the town planner.
I choose the materials, the palette
and the banners,
but don't ask me to touch a nail or a
hammer.
(sounds of work, various new
characters begin to appear)

INSPECTOR
I've come to check whether this new
Cold Coast resort
complies with the regulations - I
have to write a report.

PAULSEN
Here, just take your fee and get back
to your lowlife land of trees.

LAWYER
I think you need assistance with your
constitution and laws,
by-laws, decrees et cetera, to ensure
there are no flaws.
I have a fine knowledge of islands,
from the Bahamas to the Azores.

JUELSEN (chasing inspector and lawyer away)
Get away, what a bore!

PAULSEN
I'm in quite a state, I feel fried.
Too much excitement for one day, I
say, let's get inside.

BIRDS (chorus)
Long legs good, big wings better!
Let's take a ride together
on the wild side of extreme weather.
Long legs good, big wings better!
We're the undisputed bigwigs, kings
of the Cold Coast.
Our wing-power and nouse swept us
first past the goal post.
We're hard-nosed real-estate moguls,
poised to make a killing.

We're wheeling and dealing and we're
telling you,
we struck oil with this land of ice.
You'll have to be willing to part
with a mill or two if you want a
slice of this paradise.

Scene 5

Where a representative of the gods first appears,
manifesting their discontent.

(Paulsen enters)
PAULSEN
So the deeds are done, our accounts
are synchronized.
Soon no need to work, no unnecessary
sacrifice.
But I'm a bit surprised, there's no
word from the wall.
Has anyone heard anything at all?

GREY GOOSE (Messenger 1)
We now have a wall, a piece of
awesome stonework,
built by thousands of auks,
all their own work.

PAULSEN
Way to go, those little auks
sure walk the talk.

JUELSEN
Hey, auks don't walk, they fly,
and they don't talk, they squawk.

PINK-FOOTED GOOSE (Messenger 2)
Mr Paulsen, Mr Paulsen,

a famous tech titan has entered our
airspace,
flew straight in through the gates.
Looks like they want to challenge us
to some kind of space race.

PAULSEN
How dare they, who was it, did you
get their name?

PINK-FOOTED GOOSE
Yes, it's that upstart billionaire
with the delivery service.

PAULSEN
Why didn't you catch them and
bring 'em here?
You're making me nervous.
Get going!
(to Juelsen) I thought everything was
sorted.
What did we do to deserve this?
(helicopter approaches)

PAULSEN
Halt, who flies there? You trespass
in our air.
No drone or other delivery requests
pass here
without our blessing, do you hear?

QUEEN AMAZOOM
I'm Queen Amazoom the fly,
here on an errand from sky-high tech.
Our cloud-based trade beats your
elementary flight tech
any day. Anyway, how dare you
intercept

our delivery service?
This is unaccept…

PAULSEN
You don't unnerve us.
We're here to disrupt the industry.
We've upped the ante, we're making
history.

QUEEN AMAZOOM
Huh, don't chant victory.
When I've wrapped up
my 6-page memo to the management
team,
I'll be back.
(leaves)

BIRDS (Chorus)
We're sick of those giants from sky-
high tech
strutting around like they're
leaders of the pack.
They'll have to step back
or change their tack.
From now onwards they must interact
with us.

PAULSEN
By the way, no news from our clients
- who's keeping track?

Scene 6

In which Paulsen and Juelsen discover that some of the
gods are well-intentioned, and decide to exploit this
to their own benefit.

(enter messenger 3)
>> BARNACLE GOOSE (messenger 3)
>>> I'm back!
>>> Our ads have gone viral.
>>> Everyone's talking about "stylish
>>> survival".
>>> Everyone wants their piece of the
>>> Cold Coast, they're sold.
>>> They want to move here, invest,
>>> groove here
>>> and they're willing to pay gold.

>> PAULSEN
>>> Forget gold, we'll create our own
>>> cryptocurrency.
>>> We've got to be proactive, do or die,
>>> not just wait and see,
>>> diversify the portfolio, dynamize
>>> the deal flow.
>>> There's so much to grow, it's almost
>>> inconceivable.

>> JUELSEN
>>> Yeah, just a year ago, I'd have said
>>> unbelievable.
>>> (enter informer)

>> INFORMER
>>> Have you thought about getting some
>>> legal business protection,
>>> you know, shell companies, offshore,
>>> that kind of direction?

PAULSEN
  We don't need your advice, we're
  offshore by definition.
  Get out of here, you're under
  suspicion!
  Better leave now, of your own
  volition.
  (informer leaves, Wacky Pete enters)

PAULSEN
  Who's this now, shrouded in mystery?

WACKY PETE
  I'm from sky-high tech, but don't let
  them see me,
  I'm a dissenter, you see.
  The main thing isn't money, you need
  know-how to make history.
  I'll help you undermine their
  hegemony, if you just listen to me.
  Forget profits and hedge funds, you
  gotta share stuff for free.

PAULSEN (flattering him)
  Oh hello, it's the knowledge guru, I
  saw you on TV.
  I like your encyclopedia, seems
  pretty neat.
  I'm not sure I get all the tenets of
  your philosophy
  but if you want to share some
  insights, it'd mean a lot to me.

WACKY PETE
  Sky-high tech is driven by greed.
  A spanner in the works is what they -
  we - all need.

Let's bring them to heel, you, me and
the Cold Coasters.
I'll tell you what kind of a deal
you've got to broker.
You have to insist on sovereignty –
as an institution.
Make sure it's inscribed in the Cold
Coast constitution.
You'll be an important obstacle to
their quest for control.
Watch them start to buckle, guys,
we're on a roll.

PAULSEN (aside)
Well, of course, we could do with an
ally
and we could do worse than this
knowledge-for-all guy.
He doesn't need to know how we're
filling our purse
and he'll help us jump-start our
development growth spurt.
(to Wacky Pete)
Yes, you're right,
we need sovereignty.
We'll give them a fight.
With you on our side,
we can stand up for our rights.

Scene 7

Where the entrepreneurs trick the gods and establish
themselves as the rulers of the Cold Coast.

(a delegation of the giants of sky-high tech arrives,
speaking among themselves, accompanied by a barbarian
god and self-appointed world leader, the Triballian)

NESPECTACLE
        Rentaroom, my friend, let's approach
        them as partners.
        It'll help us open up some new
        markets.
        With four months of darkness
        it's a clear win,
        plus with minus 20 degrees
        these climate expats and retirees
        and various other middle-class
        emigrés
        will all be glued to their screens.
        We'll be able to apply truly sky-high
        fees.

RENTAROOM
        But Nespectacle,
        they're going to damage our global
        rental activities!
        Those robbers do deals dirtier than a
        one-star hotel lobby.
        They already ripped off itgothot dot
        com.

NESPECTACLE
        Nah, it'll open up more opportunities
        for income,
        from glamping on ice to - who knows -
        new sites for testing bombs.

RENTAROOM
We have to ask the Triballian.
(to Triballian) Triballian - yes or
no?

TRIBALLIAN
Co-cof-ve-veve…

RENTAROOM
See, he said no!

NESPECTACLE
He said yes!
(they argue for a while, falling
quiet when Paulsen approaches)

PAULSEN
Dear friends, so nice you're here, I
bid you welcome.
There's lots we can offer you, like
faster comms
and pole-to-pole fulfilment and
dissemination
thanks to embedded biological
navigation
systems, ensuring speedy delivery to
everyone's homes.
Our fulmars for example are far
better than drones
And we can help you build a great
entertainment zone
with guillemot karaoke via mobile
phone.
Oh, and we're also the inventors
of hyper-boreal cold data storage
centres.
Here, "in the cloud" means "under
the ice".

Basically, all goods and services
will be privatized
under our names, not yours - we'll
have full sovereignty.
But we can offer you a nice
franchise.
Wacky Pete here already told us he's
willing.

NESPECTACLE AND REST OF SKY-HIGH TECH
DELEGATION (now all convinced)
Ok, got it, that sounds fine.
(aside) Let them think they're the
big shots,
we're going to make a killing.
(to Paulsen) Where do we sign?

PAULSEN
Here, on the dotted line.

WACKY PETE (Winks to Paulsen)
We got'em this time.

PAULSEN
Yeah, neat, we bought'em.

PAULSEN AND JUELSEN (to each other)
And fooled Pete.

PAULSEN
Neat.
Plus we totally played the birds.
We made it,
who'd have thought it?

JUELSEN
Two nerds, like us...
No Amazoom or tech overlord managed
to psych us
out.

PAULSEN
Now, the treaty is signed
and sovereignty's been assigned
under Juelsen and me,
CEO and President of the Cold Coast
respectively.
We've come a long way since we first
showed up
in our modest rowboat.

JUELSEN
Yeah, me and Paulsen
have ridden an epic road.
But we're not done yet.
Stay tuned for the next episode…

BIRDS (chorus)
They all think they have the last
word:
the gods, the entrepreneurs,
even us birds. Everyone's
convinced they're slick tricksters,
sharp-witted victors.
But where do you go when you get to
the last frontier?
All we have is here.

Acknowledgements

I will be forever indebted to the people whose paths I crossed in and around Svalbard, who changed my life in small or significant ways, and who are somehow reflected in the fictional meanderings of this story. I would particularly like to mention Yann, Arne, Jørn, Annette, Bernard, Anne, Jean-Michel, Louis, Andreas and Niclas, but there are many many more.

Rosendo has been a steadfast friend for many years and a wonderful travelling companion and accomplice throughout this project, patiently putting up with my slow pace – ¡mil gracias!

I warmly thank my friends and family, especially Deanna, Sandra, Elsa, Valdas, Sacha, Jairo, Henri, Pedro and Paul, for encouraging me and for reading and commenting on various pieces and versions of this book. A special shout out to Monique for being so generous with her time, providing detailed and thoughtful feedback and forgiving me for not taking it all into account. My heartfelt appreciation also to Monica for her keen eye and expert advice regarding the design and layout of the text and illustrations.

My deepest thanks, finally, to Maya for her patience and good company, both in general and during the various lockdowns when most of this writing took place.